D1823941

"The Warrior's Heart"
Written by Justus Roux

Also by Justus Roux

Master Series:
My Master
Master's Ecstasy
Obey!
Sweet Rapture
Mistress Angelique
Wrath's Lust
Breathless (Has novella: Master Drake)
Love Thy Master
Dante and Angelique
Master Nikolai

The Demon Hunter Series:
Keeper of My Soul
Heavenly Surrender
Breathless (Has novella: Forever, Demon Hunter Ryo's story)
Ayden's Awakening

Barbarians of Malka Series:
Protector of My Heart
A Warrior's Will
A Song for My Warrior
The Warrior's Heart

Single Title
Paradise
With These Chains

Anthologies edited by Justus Roux:
Erotic Tales
Erotic Fantasy: Tales of the Paranormal
Who's Your Daddy?
Bosslady
Erotic Tales 2

Chapter One

"Zenos, you can't charge at an enemy who is much bigger than you like that," Zenith said as he easily blocked the little boy's sword.

"Yes I can. I have watched daddy fight."

"Your daddy has trained for many years. You however, have just started your training."

"Ramiro, tell Zenith to try harder. I am not afraid of being hurt."

"Your father Niro has commanded Zenith to be careful with you."

Zenos walked over to Ramiro. "Then you spar with me now," he said to the Rundal warrior.

"Afraid I can't, Zenos."

"Zenos go practice your sword swings for a little while," Zenith said as he sat down next to Ramiro.

"I want to spar!" Zenos growled, tightening his grip on his sword.

"You will do as your instructor has told."

Zenith and Ramiro quickly came up to their feet and bowed their heads as Niro entered the room. Niro was the ruler of the Dascon people and now since the unification of both the Larmat and Dascon clans he was pretty much the grand ruler of all Malka. He appointed Alistair to rule beside him as the acting leader of the Larmat people.

"But Daddy?"

"Enough!" Niro's voice thundered. "Now go do as your instructor told you to do."

"Yes Sir." Zenos quickly hurried off to practice his sword swings.

"You mustn't allow him to act like that."

"But…" Zenith kept his gaze to the ground. He was honored when Niro wanted him to help train Zenos. He suspected it was his friendship with Ramiro that help get him this position and the fact that he was only eighteen summers old. Ramiro was the Rundal leader Tomar's offspring and thankfully Zenith's best friend. Zenith was used to the Rundal's reptilian features. He has been around them since he could walk. His father Dalas was stationed at the Rundal village. In fact, he was one of the high guards of the Rundal people. A position most honored by the Dascon people.

"No excuses. I don't want my son to be a spoiled brat. He will be our next ruler someday."

"I am sorry Niro."

"There is no need to apologize."

Zenith looked up at Niro. He was always in awe being this close to the ruler of his people. Niro looked every bit the part of ruler. Strong, confident…Zenith has had the honor of training with Niro and the grand warrior Demos. Both men are idolized by all young Dascon warriors. Someday he hoped to best these men, but that was a long way off. Right now, being able to train Zenos was honor enough.

"Niro, when is my father returning from Loma?" Ramiro asked.

"That is what I would like to know. I suspect it won't be much longer." Niro missed Robin and his daughter Rose. The empress Aviva of Loma had denied any male warriors from coming to her planet. She would only speak with Robin. Nina and several Rundal warriors were escorting her. If this wasn't for his people Niro would have forbade Robin from going alone. The planet of Loma had the same problem as Malka, but only in reverse. They had a shortage of males, where as Malka had a shortage of females. More so, the Loma females were as large as the

Malka males which will make for more offspring. The Earth females, though able to mate with the warriors were almost too small to carry the large Malka infants. Robin had managed to give Niro a son and daughter, but that was all she was able to provide. Tomar had to make it so she won't be able to have any more children. The strain on her small body was too much. Niro had insisted on Tomar making this so. Robin almost died giving birth to Rose.

"Niro…" Zenith repeated. He could see Niro was lost in thought.

"What is it?" Niro forced himself to concentrate on the here and now.

"I said, your female is well guarded. I am sure everything will be fine."

"I look that worried huh?" Niro chuckled.

"Yes Sir you do."

"Zenos, you do as Zenith tells you to or I will not let you train with me later on today."

"Daddy…" Zenos rushed over. Zenos was now six summers old and looked so much like his father. Both had dark hair, full lips, dazzling green eyes, and judging by how fast Zenos was growing he would surely be just as big as his father.

Niro tussled Zenos' hair. "Another hour with Zenith and if you behave I will take you out on the training grounds with me. Today Demos is training with me."

"Really?! I will behave Daddy, I promise."

"Alright then, back to work."

Zenith watched Niro leave the room then he turned his attention back to Zenos. "Well, you get to train with your father and Demos, lucky you." He smiled down at the little boy seeing that excited look on his face.

"Yes…how do you want me to finish up my training today?"

For a six summer old boy Zenos was well spoken. Zenith suspected that was probably Robin's doing. "I think a few more sword swings should do it. You don't want to tire yourself out before you train with your father and Demos."

"Thank you Zenith. I will go over to the practice dummies and do my swings."

"You are too easy on him," Ramiro said.

"I know."

Both of them sat back down.

"You have been in a foul mood lately," Zenith said.

"It's my father. He is insisting that I choose a mate soon."

"What is so wrong about that? I would kill to have a female."

"I don't expect you to understand. With so few barbarian females you can't possibly understand my hesitation. In fact, you might want to punch me when I tell you my reasons for wanting to wait."

"What? You want to get back at your father for something?"

"It's not that simple. My father has many offspring. That is another area where the barbarians are different from my people. All offspring are basically raised by the village, not just by their parents." Ramiro stood up and moved away from Zenith just in case. Nothing was worse than an angry barbarian male. "The reason I hesitate in choosing a mate is once I have chosen a mate we are bound together forever."

"That's pretty much how my people mate."

"Yes, but…"

"You keep moving further and further away…you fear my anger…why?"

Ramiro paused. "I want to see what it is like to be with a female barbarian."

The silence hung heavy in the air.

"There are so many Rundal females. Hell, enough for every warrior to have a female. Why would you want to take one of our rare females?"

"I have been around your people since I was a hatchling." Ramiro turned toward Zenith. He was relieved that Zenith looked more puzzled than angry. "I have heard the female Rundal speak of the male barbarian's soft skin and hair. The way it's different to be taken by a barbarian than by a Rundal male. I often wondered if the male barbarian were so soft, the female must feel like heaven, silk under my scaly hands. What would it feel like to be buried deep inside such softness? I have looked at the females of your race...their beauty...the softness of their voice...the way their hips sway...the way their behind curves like it was made for a male's hands. I have felt the silky strands of their hair as they have walked by and the breeze catches their mane just so. I want to know what it's like to hold one of your females."

"I want to know that too, Ramiro. I have never been with a female, my race or yours for that matter."

"Are you angry with me?"

"No, you are just curious. The males of my people have had the pleasure of your females and you are not angry about that."

"There is no way Niro or my father for that matter would allow me to be with a female barbarian. As my father has stated the match wouldn't produce offspring. He only tolerates you male barbarians being with our females to ease their need. And probably at first out of curiosity to see if such a union would produce offspring."

"Tell your father. It can't hurt to ask."

"You don't understand. My people wouldn't allow such a union. A Rundal male is meant to protect and provide for the females. As you have stated there are many

Rundal females. I must go. It's my turn to help train the new Rundal warriors."

Ramiro left without saying anything more. Zenith sat back down and watched Zenos practiced his swings from a distance.

"You can stop now, Zenos. Have one of the guards escort you to the training grounds."

"Alright Zenith."

He smiled watching Zenos hurry off. He remembered training with his father. Hell, he still does on occasion.

A female...thoughts of holding a precious female flooded his mind. His body began to ache. His need to mate was almost unbearable now. The older he got the stronger his need for a female grew. To be a protector to a female, his female, dare he dream such a thing. He really should be angry at Ramiro for whining about choosing a mate, yet strangely he understood why Ramiro did just that. Many barbarian males sated their curiosity about the Rundal female. Was it really so wrong that a male Rundal should be curious about a female barbarian?

Zenith quickly looked up when he heard someone enter the training chamber. "Ramiro?"

"My father is sending a ship back from Loma. It should be arriving soon."

"Why do you look so excited?"

"It carries Loma warriors."

"What? More males."

"No their warriors are females. Come, I am to meet the ship. Go see if Niro will allow you to come with me."

"You want me to come with you?"

"Of course. Now hurry and go ask. I will meet you at the Conja stables."

"All right." Zenith hurried off to find Niro.

Chapter Two

Robin held little Rose in her arms as she watched Tomar and Sasha say their goodbyes. The love they had for each other showed. The bitter sweetness of their goodbye tore at Robin's heart.

Tomar wanted them all to head back to Malka. He would be staying here on Loma. Something was really wrong. Robin saw that look in his eyes. Tomar had told his warriors to take Queen Rhaya and her people to the Rundal village. Robin, Rose, Nina and a select few Loma warrior women were then to head to the barbarian village of Dascon. Niro will no doubt want them back as soon as possible. Oh God did she miss Niro and her little boy Zenos. This has been the longest time her and Niro has spent apart since they had been joined.

"Robin, you must get you and Rose inside so we can ready for launch," Nina said.

"You look so pale. Are you okay?"

"I am feeling a bit queasy that's all. I think it's this planet. It doesn't agree with me."

"I am sure once you are back in Demos' arms you will feel much better."

"Oh don't I know it. I miss the big lug something fierce. What are you looking at anyways?"

"Tomar saying goodbye to Sasha."

"Wow, they really love each other don't they. Even if they are lizard people you can still see the love between them."

"I wish they would hurry. If Empress Aviva finds out that Queen Rhaya is fleeing Loma with Adrianna and Noland we might have to fight," one of the Rundal warriors said as he gently urged the two women to get inside the ship.

Robin followed him to her seat. She secured Rose into her seat then sat down next to her. The Rundal warrior quickly secured Robin then Nina.

"Whoosh," Rose giggled.

"She likes flying in this ship doesn't she?" Nina smiled at the little girl. For a two- year-old Rose was rather large and looked more like a four-year-old. She had Niro's eyes and Robin's face. No doubt when Rose grew up she would be quite the looker.

"She loves any kind of flying. She bugs Niro to take her flying on his conja all the time."

"I can't wait to have Demos' baby. Still, it's been several years and I am still not pregnant. Demos would make such a wonderful father."

"You will have a baby. Tomar said you and Demos had nothing wrong with you."

"Yeah, but the endless gossip Demos has to endure."

"He doesn't listen to a word of it."

"I know. What man wants to hear that his mate can't have a child because she acts too much like a man."

"Oh, don't worry about it. If you notice no one ever said such things to Demos' face."

"No they don't do they. Oh man, my stomach is doing flip flops."

"Are you alright Nina?" Sasha said as she entered the chamber.

"My stomach is acting up that's all."

"You look pale and a bit tired." Sasha walked over to Nina and gently placed her hand on Nina's belly.

"Sasha, you must get ready for take off," one of the Rundal warriors said.

"Alright." She stood up and went over to one of the seats. She let the warrior strap her in. "Nina, you are with child."

"What?!"

"I feel its tiny life spark. That is why you feel tired and queasy."

"Oh, congratulations," Robin said.

"Are you sure? I don't want to get Demos' hopes up for nothing."

"Tomar has taught me well in the art of healing and medicines. I am able to sense life sparks. You are with child. Congratulations. I am sure Demos will be so happy to hear the news."

"Whoosh," Rose said again as the ship took off.

After a few moments it stabilized.

"There are so many Loma warriors coming to Rundal. A few have mates. I wish Empress Aviva will heed Tomar's warning," Sasha said.

"What warning?"

"I must tell Niro anyways so I see no harm in telling you. That sacred pool where the males magically show up on Loma…it's an anomaly."

"What?" Nina asked.

"It's a glitch in the universe. Our home planet had such a glitch. Males didn't come through it though, just strange minerals. It's this glitch that caused our planet to explode. Tomar is worried that the same fate may await Loma. The empress will not listen and ensures Tomar that the Goddess Allura wouldn't let anything happen to them."

"I take it that Queen Rhaya listened to Tomar," Robin said.

"Not on that issue. The empress wanted to destroy Queen Rhaya's village."

"What for?"

"One of the males that arrived from the glitch is from your home planet Earth. His name is Noland and he is the mate of Adrianna. He showed up with another male, but unfortunately the empress had already killed him and his mate."

"Because they were from Earth?"

"No, because Adrianna gave birth to a male child six months ago. No male child has been born on Loma in at least two centuries. The empress saw this as a bad omen and assumed that the Goddess Allura was angry with Queen Rhaya's people. I am sure there is more to it than that. Tomar hasn't gotten that far in his research."

"Is Tomar in danger?"

"Not from the empress. She sees him as some sort of deity. What I fear is that Loma may explode before the ship returns back to get my beloved."

Robin unhooked her seatbelts and hurried over to Sasha. The Rundal cried just like any human did. "It won't blow up with him on it. He wouldn't want to leave you alone. Tomar will be fine."

"His only thought was to save Queen Rhaya's people, one hundred women, about six males and six children. He wanted to save them all."

"He has. Niro will help to give them a place to live."

"I know great Niro will do all he can. If my Tomar dies, I don't know…"

"He will come back to Malka," Nina said as she hurried to Sasha.

Both women held Sasha's claws as she wept for Tomar.

౸౸౸౸

"There are so many reptilian people here," Adrianna said to Noland as they exited the ship. Her eyes widened and she clutched her baby tighter when two large male barbarian warriors approached.

"Who are they?" Noland asked as he scanned the dock. There were so many reptilian warriors and these barbarian males were growing in number as well.

"Here take little Noland." Adrianna handed the infant to him. She placed Noland behind her and drew her sword. "Stay behind me, my male."

"Wait, it is okay," Robin said as she hurried to Adrianna and the other female warriors.

"What is this?" Queen Rhaya said as she saw more large barbarian males approaching.

"They won't hurt you. They have come to greet you."

"Why are most of my people being taken to the lizard people's home? Why must we come to this barbarian land?"

"This is my home. This is Dascon. Tomar wanted you to be greeted by my mate Niro. He rules these people." Robin's heart pounded in her chest when she saw Niro approaching.

"Daddy, Daddy...Daddy?" Rose squealed as she rushed toward Niro.

Robin's smile broadened seeing Niro scooping up Rose in his arms.

"Queen Rhaya what do you want us to do?" Petra said, gripping the hilt of her sword. Petra, Mara, and Fenalla were chosen to stay with Rhaya, Adrianna and Noland. The other women were on their way to the Rundal village. Tomar thought it best if the majority of the women stayed at the Rundal village until the barbarian males had a chance to get adjusted to the Loma warrior women.

"Stand down for now. There are too many of these large male warriors."

Robin couldn't contain herself any longer and she rushed to Niro. She missed him so much and now she only wanted to feel his arms around her.

"Robin," Niro's deep voice caressed her as he scooped her up into his arms.

"I missed you so much." Robin held onto him tightly.

"I have missed you, little one." Reluctantly he set her down.

"Mommy," Zenos hurried to her.

"How is my little warrior?" Robin hugged him tightly.

"I missed you Mommy."

"Where is Nina?" Demos said as he approached.

"She is helping the Rundal warriors get the Loma people to the Rundal village. She is still in the ship."

Demos didn't say a word but headed toward the ship. Niro was about to stop him, but knew nothing would stop Demos from going to Nina.

Demos bowed his head to Queen Rhaya as he walked passed her to the ship.

"Queen Rhaya, did you see the size of that warrior," Petra said as she stood closer to Rhaya.

"Be calm."

"You must go greet Queen Rhaya," Robin whispered to Niro.

"Their warriors are larger than I expected." His eyes scanned over the large warrior women. "I don't know, Robin."

"Don't know what?"

"The Dascon male wants to protect his female. Those females are so large and strong…"

"Don't be silly. They are lovely."

"Their beauty is not in question."

"Laigne…" Rose squealed as she toddled over to Laigne. He was Robin's weaker male servant, though Robin never treated him as though he was less of a male. He was a great help to Robin.

"Shh, you must be quiet now. Robin would you like me to take Rose and Zenos back home," Laigne said.

"That would be perfect, thank you."

Laigne led the two children to the awaiting barbarian warriors. They would escort the children to the carriage. Laigne started to gather up Rose's things.

"By the Goddess," Fenalla said as her eyes locked on Laigne. Her body flooded with a desire that she was powerless to control. Fenalla was a large woman standing six feet three inches tall. Her fire red hair and piercing green eyes were envied by many Loma warrior women.

"Fenalla!" Queen Rhaya yelled as Fenalla rushed toward the group of Dascon warriors.

"Zenith!" Ramiro shouted when he saw the large woman charging toward Niro. Ramiro was forbidden to lift his sword against the Loma warriors.

Zenith drew his sword and hurried toward Niro. He stopped abruptly when Fenalla grabbed Laigne and pinned him to the ground under her. Zenith looked to Niro. Niro signaled for Zenith to sheath his sword.

"Beautiful male," Fenalla cooed as she pinned Laigne's hands above his head. She wanted him so badly. She rubbed her large body against his smaller one.

"Niro?" Robin didn't know what to do. She didn't want this woman molesting Laigne.

"Fenalla!" Queen Rhaya shouted as she and the other women hurried over. "Forgive my young warrior," she said to Niro.

"Zenith, remove her from the weaker male."

Zenith approached Fenalla and just as he was about to pull the women off the weaker male he was tackled to the ground.

"Don't touch her, barbarian," Petra growled as she placed her sword to Zenith's neck.

Zenith glared up into Petra's rich brown eyes.

"Stop this, both of you," Rhaya scolded.

Zenith bucked his body sending Petra flying over him. He grabbed her legs, flipped her over and pinned her under him. He squeezed her wrist until she released her sword.

"Stop this!" Robin yelled.

"Zenith release the female."

Zenith quickly stood up and stepped back. Petra leapt up to her feet as she scooped up her sword. She was surprised by the strength of the male warrior.

"Enough of this. You are my guests. My people mean you no harm. I ask that you keep your swords sheathed unless of course you are training. Now let me escort you to where you will be staying. We have much to discuss."

Fenalla stood up and pulled Laigne up to his feet, she then threw him over her shoulder.

"Niro…" Robin whispered. She wanted that warrior woman's hands off of Laigne. She had no right to take Laigne like that. Robin never allowed Laigne to be used by the male Dascon warriors and she sure the hell wasn't about to let these women use him.

"Queen Rhaya, please have your warrior release my mate's servant."

"Do as King Niro has said."

Reluctantly Fenalla put Laigne down. She wanted to claim this male for her own, right now.

"Just call me Niro."

"You may address me as Rhaya."

Robin loved to watch Niro. He was born to be a leader. Added to that his father Hakan's teaching, it all made Niro a grand leader. She couldn't be prouder of her mate.

Petra glared at Zenith. How dare this barbarian male even think of touching a Loma warrior.

"Petra, let's go," Rhaya said as she gently grabbed her arm.

"Yes, my Queen." Petra sheathed her sword. Her eyes were still locked on Zenith.

"Whoa, she don't like you," Ramiro whispered as he stood next to Zenith.

"She will get over it." Zenith returned her venomous looks. Only when Petra was out of sight did Zenith relax. "Did you see the one with fire hair attack that weaker male?"

"Well, it's no surprise. Those smaller males are what are prized on Loma."

"Phhh, why? What female wouldn't want a strong male to protect her and her young."

"A female capable of protecting herself." Ramiro was most intrigue by the large warrior females. Never had he seen females so strong before. Not even Nina, Demos' mate could match these warrior women's veraciousness. If gossip was continually spread about Nina being a warrior, wait until word about the Loma warriors start to fly.

"They were beautiful though." Zenith adjusted his sword strap.

"That they were."

"Though a female should be smaller."

"I bet the Loma females are thinking the same thing about you barbarian males about now." Ramiro chuckled.

ಖುಖುಖು

Nina escorted the last Loma warrior to the awaiting carriages. There were too many of them to simply take the conjas. When Queen Rhaya was ready, her and her escorts would fly on the conjas to the Rundal village.

Demos watched her from a distance. Even in the mist of much larger and stronger female warriors Nina stood out. Her presence, the way she carried herself. Damn he could look at her all day. His body missed hers so much that it ached with need. He hated being away from her. When she turned around and caught sight of him. That smile on her face almost took his breath away.

"Demos!" she cried out as she rushed toward him.

He was frozen in place. The only thing he could do was open his arms, awaiting her. Nina threw herself in his arms. He wrapped his arms around her tightly and held her as close as he could. He carried her behind one of the large pillars in the corner. He hoped that it would block anyone's view of them. At this moment he didn't care whether someone spotted them or not. All he knew is that his body needed hers. He set her down and began removing his loincloth.

"What are you doing?" Nina looked around making sure no one was watching.

"I need you, my female." He pulled on the strings of her pants causing them to fall from her body.

"Someone will see us. We should wait until…"

He lifted her up and opened her legs. With one strong thrust he rammed his cock deeply into her.

"Ahhh," Nina moaned. "Demos…" His large cock filled and stretched her. The urgent way he took her was intoxicating. All she could do was wrap her arms and legs around him as he drove his cock harder and deeper into her.

"My female, oh my sweet female," he growled.

"Yes, Demos, yes." She tried to muffle her cries by biting her lip. Her body trembled as her pleasure mounted. His scent, his skin, his voice, oh his sweet cock, all of him, she could feel his very essence as he continued to drive himself into her.

"Take your pleasure, female. I need to take my…Nina," his deep voice growled sending her over the edge.

She gazed at him as he arched back and roared his orgasm. She no longer cared who heard. Her body quivered seeing that look of bliss on his face, feeling his cum fill her.

He held her tightly. "I love you, Nina," he whispered.

"I love you, my male."

He held her close for a few moments then reluctantly let her down. They both quickly put their clothes back on. He stared into her beautiful face. She had something to tell him he could see it in her eyes.

"What is it?" He wasn't sure if it was good or bad news she had for him.

"I…I should tell you later. I have to get the Loma warriors off to the Rundal village."

"The Rundal warriors are more than capable of doing that task. Tell me, come on female, I know you want to tell me something."

"I was never too good at keeping things from you." She grabbed his hand. "I'm pregnant," she said softly.

"What?" Demos grabbed her other hand.

"I am going to have your kid." She smiled up at him. That look on his face took every fear she had away.

"Are you certain?" His voice filled with excitement.

"Sasha said I was pregnant."

Demos grabbed her and lifted her up high as he roared out his battle cry. "I am going to be a father!"

"You better put me down, you big lug."

Demos carefully set her down as if she was made of glass. "My female," he gently said as he caressed her cheek.

"I can safely assume you are happy with my news."

"No male could be happier."

They left the corner and ignored the small group of people who had gathered to see what all the commotion was about.

"You must be careful now. I must be careful with you," Demos said squeezing her hand tightly.

"Don't treat me like a fragile thing. I know what my body can handle."

"Sasha or Tomar will determine that."

"But…" She decided not to argue right now. Demos was too happy. "I bet you want a son, don't you?"

"No, I want a daughter, a female just like you, strong, beautiful, talented…just like you."

"Well, I want a son, a male just like you."

"One of me is enough."

Nina couldn't understand why Demos didn't think more of himself. He has proven himself to be one of the best warriors on this planet. His loyalty to Niro and his people was unmatched, not to mention he has been a wonderful mate to her, and she had no doubt he would be a great father. She knew that scar that ran across his eye bothered him, but it took nothing away from his beauty. Nothing could ever do that.

"You must rest now."

"I feel fine. I have to get the Loma warriors on their way."

Demos led her to where the Loma warrior women were being loaded up into the carriages. He walked up to one of the Rundal warriors. "I would like to take my female home. I am sure you and your warriors can handle this task."

"Certainly Demos."

"See, they are capable of escorting these warriors."

Nina looked out at the warrior women. All of them were staring at Demos with a cautious eye. It was quite obvious that it was going to take some time for the Loma and the Dascon warriors to get use to each other.

"Now let's go home. My presence is making the Loma warriors uneasy."

"Okay." Nina decided not to argue. In truth she was feeling a bit tired. But there was no way she was going to tell him that.

"We will send a report to Niro once the Loma people have been settled in," the Rundal warrior said to Demos.

"I will let Niro know."

Demos smiled down at Nina. He was going to be a father. He thought his heart might just burst. He gently took her hand and led her out of the terminal. He had to get her home so she could rest.

Chapter Three

Petra looked out across the Dascon village from the balcony of her chamber. She was glad for the lizard males they saved Queen Rhaya from the empress, but at the same time she wasn't too happy about being surrounded by all these barbarian male warriors. Since she was a girl she has heard the stories about the history of Loma. How when the males ruled war raged constantly until the Goddess Allura cursed the males by sending a disease to destroy almost all of them. There were no more strong male warriors anymore on Loma. The Goddess gave the task of defending Loma to the females. It had been that way for some time. Females grew larger and stronger and to ensure this continued the Goddess sent smaller males to them through the sacred pond. This would continue until the day a male was born to a Loma warrior and one of these sacred males.

Petra was excited when Adrianna gave birth to a male child. This meant the Goddess had forgiven the male warriors and soon more males would be born on Loma. She was confused when the empress saw the birth of little Noland to symbolize that the Goddess was angry with Queen Rhaya and her people. Nowhere in the legends did it say that a male child was a curse.

The lizard males saved her village and for that she would always be indebted to them. However, could she trust these barbarian males?

The image of the young male warrior she engaged while protecting Fenalla popped into her mind. She couldn't deny he was a beautiful male. That long dark hair, and those dark eyes that burnt with such fire. He was beautiful and very strong. Zenith, the leader of the barbarians address the young warrior as, it suited him. Ah, she couldn't think about that warrior. She had to focus on protecting her queen. The lizard male said these barbarians wouldn't harm them. But she had to be certain of this.

"You seemed distressed," Mara said. Mara had trained with Petra and they were good friends. Mara was just as big as Petra both stood six foot two, both had dark hair though Petra's was rather long while Mara's was only shoulder length. Both were honored being one of the queen's guards.

"That damn barbarian warrior. I wish our queen would have let me teach that ox a lesson."

"Oh really, that's all you are thinking about."

"What does that mean?"

"You have to admit that male was rather attractive."

"What does that have to do with anything?"

"Plenty I would say. I don't know about you, but I could use a male's body. With only a few sacred males a year coming from the Goddess, it gets mighty lonely. This planet has plenty of males."

"Yeah, big loud obnoxious ones."

"Who probably have very large cocks."

"Stop that." Petra playfully punched Mara.

"Fenalla is all wound up about that little male. She is busy asking the queen if she can hunt him."

"He was really cute."

"That he was."

"I doubt the queen is going to let Fenalla do anything with that male anyways."

"No, probably not, but you know Fenalla, when she wants something she finds a way to get it."

"That's Fenalla." Petra chuckled.

"Speaking of." Mara motioned to the door.

"Hey you two, the queen wants us to go out to these barbarian training ground and train. She wants these males to see what we can do."

"Who will guard the queen?" Petra asked.

"The lizard males."

"I could use a little training. It was a long flight over here," Mara said.

The women gathered their swords and headed for the training grounds.

ഇരുത്തെ

"You are too slow, Ramiro," Zenith said as he dodged yet another one of Ramiro's attacks.

"That may be, but unlike you I do more than just practiced."

"Well, if I was as weak as you I would pursue other interest too."

"Weaker huh?" Ramiro swung his sword and connected with Zenith's, causing both swords to vibrate.

"Now that's better. What are you looking at?" Zenith turned around to see what Ramiro was gazing at. "It's those damn Loma warriors, what the hell do they think they are doing out here."

"I suspect they want to train." Ramiro sheathed his sword and started walking over to the females. Zenith grabbed his arm to stop him.

"Where are you going?"

"To make the females feel welcome."

"Well, good luck with that. Look around, I would say that none of the males are too happy having females on the training grounds."

"This male doesn't mind." Ramiro freed his arm from Zenith and continued walking to the females.

"Ah, it's a lizard male," Petra said as she watched Ramiro come closer.

"He looks different than the others," Mara said.

"He looks like all the other lizard males to me."

"Good morning warriors," Ramiro greeted them. "I am called Ramiro."

"Good morning Ramiro," the three females said.

"I see these barbarian males are already having a problem with us wanting to train."

"Tell me something. Would you allow the males from your planet to come out here and train with you?"

"Of course not," Fenalla quickly said.

"Well, these males wouldn't want their females coming out here and training, and since you are females."

"Oh…well they are just going to have to get over it." Petra drew her sword.

"I will challenge you first," Fenalla said as she drew her sword.

"Ramiro may I ask you something?" Mara said.

"You may ask me anything."

"Your skin, it has a slight purple hue to it. The other lizard males I have seen are more blackish-grey. Even Tomar was colored as them."

"My people come in various colors. Generally the males are blackish in color with grey, blue and purple hue. The females are greenish in color with yellowish, gold and sometimes a slight bluish hue."

Mara moved her hand tenderly down Ramiro's arm. "Still, you have such lovely skin and you are softer than the other lizard males."

"My people are called Rundal, not lizard."

"Oh, I'm sorry."

"Don't worry about it. You have touched other Rundal males?"

"Yes, they were kind enough to sate my curiosity. Your people's skin looks like it would feel rubbery, but it really doesn't. You may touch me if you like."

"Excuse me?"

"The other lizard…umm…I mean Rundal males wanted to touch me. So I thought you might like to."

Ramiro timidly reached out his hand. Though the top of his hand was a bit scaly, his palm was just like a human's. He slowly ran his hand down Mara's arm. Her skin was so soft, yet firm. He could feel the slight muscle lines of her arms as his fingers slowly ran down the length of her arm. He reluctantly pulled his hand away, even though he wanted nothing more than to feel the rest of her body.

He looked into her eyes when he felt the heat from her stare. That look in her eyes made his cock instantly hard. She had enjoyed his touch and was obviously aroused. He could smell her arousal, hell he could see her lust dancing in her eyes.

"I must go back to training." He turned and walked away he had to get away from her. No human female ever looked at him the way Mara had just done. He had his fair share of Rundal females look at him with that kind of lust in their eyes, but never a human female.

"Are you alright?" Zenith asked.

"I will be. Is Niro coming out to practice soon?"

"I believe so."

"I hope so. The male warriors won't take these females out here training for too much longer."

"You!"

Zenith's eyes locked with Petra's as she approached them.

"My name is Zenith. What do you want female?"

"Train with me."

"I don't train with females."

"Afraid I will kick your ass."

Zenith drew his sword and approached Petra.

The fire in his eyes was so sexy. Petra gripped her sword tighter.

"If I hurt you, you better not start crying," Zenith said.

"Don't worry I won't. But...if I win you must do what I ask."

"Fine, whatever, you won't win." Zenith charged at her. He couldn't think about her being a female, she was just another warrior at this moment.

A large group of males started to gather as Zenith and Petra's match went on. She was much better than he gave her credit for. This surprised the hell out of him, yet at the same time intrigued him.

"You are pretty good, male."

"You're not too bad yourself, female."

"Zenith, be careful," Ramiro said.

"Don't worry lizard male, this barbarian won't hurt me." Petra charged at Zenith.

"What's going on?" Demos said as he and Niro entered the training grounds.

"Let's go see."

"Great Niro, those Loma females are out here," one of the barbarian warriors said as he approached Niro.

"Really? Is that what's going on over there?"

"Zenith is sparring with one of the females."

"I would like to see this," Demos said.

They went over and watched the match.

Zenith swung his sword catching the string to Petra's top, pulling it from her. She made no attempt to cover herself, but instead continued fighting. Zenith's eyes were drawn to her ample breasts. The next thing he knew he was looking up at the sky with Petra's sword at this neck.

"That's the problem with you males. You are easily distracted."

Petra climbed off Zenith and took the towel Demos handed her. Every male was looking at her.

"Oh for heaven sakes, it's just my breasts, not some holy artifact."

Ramiro helped Zenith to his feet.

"Well male, it looks like you owe me my prize."

"Looks that way. I shouldn't have allowed myself to be distracted."

"It's good to know you can admit your mistake."

"What do you want?"

"I want to see your body."

A collective gasp rang out amongst the males.

"They don't act like females should," a male warrior said. Several males agreed.

"How should a female act?" Petra walked over to the large male.

"Delicate, demure, modest, no warrior wants his female to be seen by others and certainly doesn't want his female to speak as you do."

"Really? On Loma, it's the males who are delicate, demure, modest and in need of protecting."

"Weaker males," one male said as he spat on the ground.

"Our males are not weak," Fenalla added.

"Niro, give these bitches the weaker males. Maybe they will go back home."

"Enough!" Niro's voice boomed. "Forgive my warriors rudeness."

The three women bowed their heads to Niro.

"But you must understand Malka is just like Loma, but only in reverse. So I ask that you give my warriors time to adjust."

"Yes great Niro."

"Please just call me Niro. Now you may train on this training ground, but I ask that you stay on your corner of it."

"Thank you Niro."

"The rest of you get back to your training."

Petra waited for Niro to leave. "Zenith, I want my prize."

"You can't be serious."

"I am very serious." She looked around then spotted a series of smaller huts. "What are those for?"

"Those are for storage."

"Follow me."

"Why?"

"I want my prize."

Zenith followed her to one of the storage huts. They stepped inside and she sat down on some crates.

"You want to see my body?"

"Yep, now take off that loincloth."

Zenith didn't know what to think. He was aroused, yet repulsed, angry, yet excited...slowly he removed his loincloth and let it fall to the floor. That look on her face made his cock instantly hard.

She stood and walked over to him. "You are so large." She fell to her knees and took his cock into her mouth.

"Ah...WH...at..." Zenith started breathing hard. Her mouth was so warm, wet, and the movement of her tongue, the sucking...just seeing his cock in her mouth and that look on her face.

"Oh damn you taste so sweet." She ran her tongue up and down his cock. Her hand kneaded his balls as the other reached back and grabbed his ass.

Zenith couldn't stop himself from grabbing her head and thrusting his hips. His eyes were locked on her. She sucked and slurped, licked and swallowed all of him. He felt his orgasm building.

"I am going to come," he panted.

"Mmmm," she growled.

Her growls sent him over the edge, his cum exploded from his body. She drank down every drop then caressed his cock with her tongue.

"Damn you taste so good." She stood up and started to lick her fingers.

Zenith lifted her up and laid her down across the crates. He pulled her pants from her, and then buried his face in her pussy. He needed to taste her, needed to bring her the pleasure she just had given him.

"Stop Zenith…bury your cock in me."

He jumped up to his feet and grabbed her hips. He drove his cock deeply into her. The feeling of her pussy engulfing his cock was nirvana. She was so tight, warm and wet. He growled almost like an animal as he drove himself deeper and faster into her.

"Harder, oh yeah like that."

He gripped her hips tighter, driving himself harder and harder until he couldn't hold back the wave of pleasure anymore. He roared out his orgasm then collapsed onto her. He felt her arms and legs wrap around him, holding him tightly to her.

"That was better than I thought it would be," she said quietly.

He arched up and looked down into her face.

"My planet has so few males that only the lucky females ever get to feel a male's body like this. I am sorry if…"

Zenith placed his finger on her lip to silence her. "My planet has too few females…this is my first time with a female."

Petra couldn't help but smile. He was her first male.

"Thank you," he said softly as he caressed her cheek.

Petra heard Mara calling for her.

"I better go see what she wants."

Zenith pulled his cock from her and then reached down and handed her, her pants. He walked over and scooped up his loincloth. "You can use my body whenever you want while you are here," he said quietly.

"Do you mean that?"

"Yes." He felt so awkward.

"Thank you," she said then she left.

He quickly put on his loincloth. He didn't really know what to think at this moment. Everything happened so fast. His body felt sated for the moment. He finally had the pleasure of a female. Now he knew why the males lucky enough to be a protector or mate to a female were so protective of them and why they treated them like precious treasures.

Zenith went back out to the training grounds. He had to train Zenos today so he better clear his head. He hoped that Demos would do him the honor of sparring with him.

Chapter Four

Laigne carefully folded the silky fabric. Robin was having new coverings made for her and Rose today. She carefully chose the fabrics and colors she wanted.

Laigne enjoyed taking care of Robin and her children. Over the years Robin has tried hard to change the way weaker males were treated on Malka. She was making some progress here in Dascon, but the Larmat people were proven to be difficult. After all they simply killed any male child that didn't grow up strong. Thank goodness Alistair banned that practice, but still he couldn't be everywhere all the time and certainly not in every village.

Laigne smiled remembering the excitement in Robin's eyes when she heard about the Loma warriors and how they treasured weaker males. Niro however only saw the new females as more to give to his worthy warriors. Laigne knew Niro basically put up with him because Robin likes him so much. He didn't care. As long as he could stay here with Robin and the children he was happy.

"Laigne, would you make sure the cooks are preparing traditional Loma dishes for our guests. I would go down there myself, but this fitting is taking longer than I thought," Robin said.

"No problem." He put down the fabric and headed out of the room. Robin fussed over every detail of important functions. Yet another thing Laigne liked about her. She always made her guests feel welcomed.

Half way to the cooking area Laigne couldn't shake the feeling that he was being watched. He looked around everywhere and couldn't see anything. There were a couple large male warriors right ahead of him. Instinctively he tried to stay out of their sight. It was forbidden for any male warrior to use Laigne like they used the other weaker males, but if the warrior was horny enough rules matter little. His eyes darted over to another male servant who was busy cleaning the banisters of the large balcony. Then his gaze quickly went back to the male warriors. One of them was heading toward the servant. Laigne started to feel sick to his stomach at the thought of what was about to happen to the weaker male. He quickly looked away when the warrior grabbed the weaker male and pulled him to one of the rooms.

The familiar anger started to boil inside him. It wasn't males' fault that they weren't born strong or large. Why was it okay for the larger males to treat the smaller ones like this?

His heart started to pound in his chest when he heard the heavy footsteps of a large male warrior approaching him. He took a deep breath and started to walk forward. His breath caught when he felt the strong hand grab his arm tightly.

"I want my cock sucked, weaker male."

"Niro has forbidden the use of me to any warrior," Laigne quietly said.

"Niro isn't here right now and if you say anything to him I will have to kill you. Now come here." The large male pulled Laigne close to him. "On your knees right now and suck my cock until I find release."

"No!" Laigne tried to fight the large warrior.

"Do you honestly believe you can stop me." The warrior pushed Laigne down to his knees. "Do what I have told you. Right now, weaker male."

Laigne felt the bile rise up. He stopped struggling and accepted his fate. Maybe, this male will simply be satisfied with having his cock sucked and just go away afterwards.

Before the male had time to remove his loincloth he was knocked to the ground. It happened so fast Laigne couldn't see what had happened at first. He quickly came up to his feet and moved to the side.

"Stay there, this male won't harm you," Fenalla said to Laigne.

"You fucking bitch. Very well..." The male jumped back up to his feet and grabbed his sword. "Once I have defeated you I will fuck the hell out of you, then I will make that pitiful weaker male suck me off."

"You won't lay a finger on him."

Fenalla charge the large male. Laigne looked around for anything he could use to help her. It was suicide to strike one of those large male warriors, but he couldn't let the female fight him alone. His eyes disparately scanned everywhere.

"Just stay where you are little male," Fenalla said as she kicked the male warrior square in the balls. He fell to the floor coughing and gasping.

She went over to Laigne and picked him up throwing him over her shoulder. She took off running.

"Whoa, that was a strong male. This is our best course of action," she said as she carried Laigne to another part of the leader hut. When she thought they had enough distance between them and the large male warrior she set Laigne down.

"Are you okay?" she asked looking him over.

"Yes," he said quietly unable to look her in the eyes.

"Is this normal?"

"Is what normal."

"For the large males to simply force themselves on the smaller ones."

"Yes. It is their right."

"Right? To take someone against their will. May I ask you something rather personal?"

"Alright."

"Do you enjoy being with another male?"

"No…"

"This is not right. No warrior has a right to take what is not his or hers for that matter. So, I must apologize to you for what I done the first time I met you."

"There is no need for that." Laigne looked up into her beautiful face. My God she was beautiful too. Her flaming red hair framed her pretty face and those emerald green eyes were the most gorgeous eyes he had ever seen.

"It's just that you are perfect and I couldn't control myself. I have never had the privilege of touching a male before."

"Me…perfect…" Laigne couldn't help but chuckle. "I am sure your view on perfect will change once you have been here awhile. The females on this planet want those large, strong warriors and not some one like me."

Fenalla moved closer to him. "To me, you are perfect. Your face has such life, you are so pretty, delicate, soft spoken." She ran her fingers through his shoulder length dark hair. "Your hair is so soft and your eyes, your dark beautiful eyes are mesmerizing."

Laigne stepped away from her.

"Perhaps it's me you don't find attractive," she said.

"You…"

"I know I am larger than your females. My body is strong and probably not as soft. I will never be dainty or demure and I won't sheath my sword and stay in the hut…"

"You are beautiful. Much more than a weaker male like me deserves."

"You are no weaker male."

"Fenalla." Queen Rhaya walked up to her. "I thought I told you to leave this male alone."

"She protected me from one of the male warriors."

"Is this so?"

"Yes, my Queen."

Rhaya motioned to two of the Rundal warriors.

"Yes, your highness," they both said in unison.

"Please escort this male to where he needs to go."

"Thank you, my Queen," Fenalla said.

"Thank you, Fenalla," Laigne said as he walked off with the Rundal warriors.

"I know you desire that small male, Fenalla, but Niro has asked you to leave that male alone. It upsets his mate."

"I know, but…"

"However, I see no harm in you speaking with him, if he doesn't mind."

"Thank you, my Queen."

"I want you to find Mara and Petra. We have much to discuss today."

"I will find them right away."

ಬಂಬಂಬಂ

Niro paced around his chamber. He was meeting with Queen Rhaya. He was at a loss on what to think about the Loma warriors. He wasn't expecting them to be so large. When Tomar said the females were warriors he quite honestly believed they would be like Nina.

"Daddy?" Zenos hurried over to him.

"You shouldn't be in here."

"Mommy said I could for a little while."

"What is it that you want?"

"Saa is here and so too is Demos."

"Oh I see now. You can stay for a few moments."

"Niro," Saa said as he entered the chamber. A beautiful little girl stayed close to him. "Flora wanted to play with Zenos. I saw no harm in bringing her."

"Flora." Zenos walked over to the little girl. She was about a year and half younger than him.

"Zenos." She let go of Saa's hand and grabbed Zenos' hand.

"How is Sabrina?" Niro asked.

"She is almost ready to give birth to my son. Tomar said this is the last child she can give me."

"It is safer this way. The Earth females are just too small to have more than two children." Niro watched Zenos playing carefully with Flora. "Flora will be a very beautiful female when she has grown up."

"That she will be, she looks just like her mother," Saa said with much pride in his voice. "She will make a fine match for Zenos."

"Yes she will."

"Demos," Saa greeted Demos as he entered the chamber.

"What's with that look on your face?" Niro asked.

"I am a happy male. Nina is with child."

"About time." Saa slapped Demos on the back.

"Do you know if it's male or a female child yet?" Niro asked.

"Not yet. It doesn't matter as long as the child and Nina get through this healthy."

"Niro, Queen Rhaya is here," a young male warrior said.

"Show her in."

"I have seen these Loma warriors. They are much larger than I thought they would be," Saa said.

"I know."

"Our warriors will only want to sate their lust with them. I don't know how many would want such a large female as a mate."

"Our warriors are in no position to be so picky about their mates," Demos added.

"Zenos take Flora into the other room," Niro said.

"I will protect her, Daddy." Zenos gently grabbed Flora's hand and led her to the other room.

"That is so precious."

Niro quickly looked behind him hearing Robin's voice.

"What are you doing here?"

"I thought Queen Rhaya might feel more comfortable with a female present."

Niro caressed her cheek. "You are a wise female."

The young male warrior escorted Rhaya, Petra, Mara and Fenalla in, then he left the room.

"Please be seated," Niro said, gesturing to a large table that had a map covering it.

"Fenalla, go get Adrianna and Noland."

"Yes, my Queen."

"Niro, I am sure Tomar's mate has told you about our circumstance by now."

"Yes, she has."

"Then you already know my people can't return to Loma."

"I understand."

"I can also see in your eyes that my warriors are not what you were expecting and to be honest your warriors are much larger than I had anticipated. However, I believe in what Tomar had discussed with me. I think our people can produce many offspring together. But, it will take some time for trust to build between us."

"My warriors have been lonely for some time. And I fear they might start to treat your warriors as they do the weaker males. I am sure Tomar has explained our culture to you."

"Yes he has. That is what I wish to discuss with you."

"I think we are on the same train of thought. I don't want your people to feel unwelcome, but I feel it might be best if you stay in the Rundal village for the time being. You need to be with your people and my warriors need time to adjust as I am sure so does yours. I would like to send some of my finest younger warriors to escort you to the Rundal village." Niro paused when Fenalla escorted Adrianna and Noland in. He was taken back by the image before him. Noland had the baby cradled in his arms and Adrianna was standing protectively by his side.

"This is how my people live. The female protects and the male nurtures. It has been this way for a couple of centuries now. This small male child has turned Loma upside down. He was supposed to be a symbol of hope and somehow the empress has turned him into a curse. Niro, I don't know if you can understand what I am trying to say."

"Alistair," Niro whispered.

"Excuse me."

"You said that baby was your planets symbol of hope. I can understand what you mean. Alistair the male who helps me rule Malka is this planet's symbol of hope. He is the offspring of a Larmat father and a Dascon mother. He is seen as a curse by some and hope by others. So yes, I do know what you are saying."

Rhaya smiled at Niro.

Robin went over to Noland and looked at the small baby he was holding. "He is beautiful." She gazed into Noland's eyes. "Where were you from?"

"United States, Arizona to be more précised."

"I am from the United States too."

"Really?"

Adrianna looked down at Noland. He looked excited to see someone from his home planet.

"We will have to talk sometime while you are here," Robin said.

"I would like that very much."

Robin walked back over to Niro.

"Niro, I would like to leave Adrianna and Noland here. Plus I would like to leave Fenalla to guard them. If this is alright with you? I think it would be best for my people to get adjusted to what has happened to them and some might find fault with Adrianna."

"Why would they find fault with her?"

"She is the one who had the male child."

"I see. This would be fine."

"Then I would like to leave right away to the Rundal village. I am eager to ease the minds of my people."

"I will have everything ready for you to leave in the morning."

Rhaya stood up. "I have hope that our people can learn to live together. You are not what I expected."

"What did you expect?"

"An overbearing brute of a male. But to my surprise you are nothing like that at all. I look forward to meeting with you again."

Niro watched them leave.

"She is what I expected."

"Really?" Robin asked.

"I thought she would be like you, my female. Strong, compassionate and soft spoken." Niro stood. "Have Ramiro choose six young male warriors to accompany him and the Loma warriors to the Rundal village." Niro instructed one of his warriors.

"Yes Sir."

Niro lifted Robin up and kissed her softly then he set her down. He stroked her hair gently. "I must see to their safe journey. But later..." He smiled and softly growled at her.

"Mmmm," was all she said.

"Come Demos and Saa we must ready them for their journey."

"I will watch Flora for you, Saa," Robin said.

"My thanks."

Robin watched them leave. Her body was already anticipating Niro's touch. It seem like every year they been together it only made her want him more. She doubted she would ever tire of his touch.

She walked over to the next room and smiled watching Zenos and Flora play together.

Chapter Five

Zenith readied his things for the trip. He was rather excited about seeing the Rundal village again. He was eager to see his father and mother. He couldn't stop thinking about Petra. How soft and wonderful her body felt. His cock started to harden at just the mere thought of her. He quickly tried to focus on something else.

Ramiro peeked his head inside Zenith's chamber. "I will meet you at the docks. Hurry up, the ship is almost ready."

"I am almost done. I will be at the docks in five minutes." He heard Ramiro leave. He threw a couple more things into his bag and was almost ready to leave. He was startled when the door flew open.

"Zenith."

Zenith quickly turned around and bowed his head to Niro. "Sir."

"I want you to give this note to your father."

"I will Sir." Zenith took the note from Niro.

"Hurry up Zenos, Zenith has to get going."

Zenith watched as Zenos stepped out from behind Niro.

"I will practice what you have taught me while you are gone. I promise."

Zenith smiled. Zenos was going to miss him he could see it in the little boy's face. Zenos was trying hard to be brave in front of Niro.

"I expect to see that your swings have gained strength by time I get back."

"That means you are coming back?"

"Of course I am." Zenith could see how awkward Zenos felt. "Here." He pulled a small dagger out of his bag. "I have asked the weapons maker to make a holster for this. It should be ready within the week." Zenith handed Zenos the dagger. "You have to start learning to battle with this strapped to your leg. A warrior must always have a back up just in case his sword is render useless in battle."

"Thank you," Zenos said quietly as he carefully took the dagger. Tears started to form in Zenos' eyes. The whole time he had been training Zenith has been his teacher.

"That is a fine blade son," Niro said as he tousled Zenos' hair. "You will have to train with me while Zenith is gone."

"Really?"

"Well, you still have to train don't you."

Zenith saw the sadness start to leave Zenos' face.

"Now we must let Zenith finish getting ready. Make sure your father gets that note."

"I will."

Zenos ran over to Zenith then stopped. He was unsure of what he should do. He wanted to hug Zenith to say goodbye, but he wasn't sure he should in front of Niro.

Zenith did the warrior salute to Zenos. Zenos quickly did it back.

"Come Zenos. Take care Zenith."

"Yes Sir."

Zenith finished packing then hurried to the landing pad. They were going to take conjas, but Queen Rhaya refused to ride the strange winged creature. Luckily a small Rundal ship had arrived to gather some supplies for the village.

"About time," Ramiro said as Zenith approached.

"Zenos wanted to say goodbye."

"That's sweet."

"Pfff…"

"What's with that noise?"

"You Rundal males…let's get going."

"What do you mean, you Rundal males."

"No barbarian male would say what you just did."

"Oh please, give me a break." Ramiro grabbed his bag and headed with Zenith to the ship. "The Loma women are already on board."

"What of the one called Petra?"

"She's there. Why?" Ramiro said teasingly.

"No reason. Don't even start."

They handed their bags to one of the Rundal males then boarded the ship. Zenith found himself eagerly looking forward to seeing Petra. This kind of bugged him. She wasn't his mate, she probably wouldn't be either. He was only eighteen summers old far too young to be a female's protector. The older more experience warriors would probably defeat him in a battle to be her protector. Generally, a male usually reaches his mid twenties before he is skilled enough to be a female's protector. Even then, it was a hard battle to stay her protector.

"I was hoping the lizard male would choose you to come with us."

Zenith felt Petra's hands caress his ass.

"Follow me."

He didn't say a word as he followed her to the cargo hold. She pulled at the ties to his loincloth. He quickly helped her remove it. She stepped out of her pants and laid on top of one of the crates.

"We must hurry."

Zenith grabbed her and lifted her from the crate. He turned her around then bent her over the crate. He grabbed her hips and drove his cock deeply into her. When she tried to raise her head he pushed her head back down. He wanted her like this. Like a protector would take his mate. He leaned over when she tried to arch up. He bit her shoulder and used his weight to pin her to the crate as he drove his cock deeper and faster into her.

Petra tried to free herself, but was unable to move him. She felt his teeth bite down a little harder. When he started to growl like an animal she felt a shudder rush through her body. Her pussy grew wetter the louder he growled. She liked this, liked having him be the dominant one. It went against everything she was taught. A female was in control, a male was the passive one. Not Zenith, oh God, not Zenith. She surrendered to him which caused him to growl louder and thrust harder. Her whole body quivered from her orgasm.

"Yesss!!!" he practically howled as his orgasm slammed him.

He gently kissed where he had bitten her. Luckily he didn't break the skin.

"I'm sorry…"

"Don't you apologize that was wonderful," Petra said. "We must hurry and get back to the others."

Quickly they got dressed and headed to where the others were being strapped down to their chairs.

"Where did you go?" Mara asked when Petra sat next to her. She looked up and saw Zenith as he sat next to Ramiro. "Never mind, I can figure it out." She smiled at Petra.

"I don't even want to know where you have been," Ramiro said to Zenith.

"As close to paradise as I can be," Zenith said winded.

"Is everyone on board?" a Rundal male said.

"I believe so," Ramiro responded. He looked over at Mara. That smile on her face was teasing him. She wanted him. There was no mistaking her intentions. If he could see it surely others can. Her eyes caressed his body, making his body tighten.

"Well, you may sate your curiosity after all," Zenith whispered to him.

"What do you mean?" Ramiro shifted nervously in his seat.

"That other Loma warrior wants you. Don't tell me you didn't notice."

"Let's focus on getting to the Rundal village."

Zenith didn't say another word as the ship took off.

Chapter Six

Tomar studied the scrolls he found in the ancient library of Loma. The empress was being most cooperative, a fact Tomar was grateful for. He needed to know how long that anomaly was on this planet. On the home planet of Rundal, the anomaly was only there about fifty years before it became unstable. Tomar needed to know if it was the minerals that came through that caused his planet to be destroyed. From everything he has read the Loma anomaly has been here for at least two hundred years.

"Great lizard male," a young warrior said as she entered the room. "I have brought you food and drink."

"Thank you." He cleared some of the papers as she set the tray down. "Tell me is there more scrolls other than what's in this library?"

"The empress has the royal collection. But only those with royal blood may read them."

"Again thank you for the food." He waited until she left then he headed to another room in the library. This room was sealed off. The key opening looked like the pendant the empress wore around her neck.

"Lizard male have you found what you are looking for?"

Tomar quickly turned around hearing the empress' voice

"Not yet. But if I could make a request, I would like to look at the royal collection if this is possible."

"You may not understand the meaning of the scrolls."

"I would like to try if you would allow it."

Aviva took off her necklace and used it to open the door. "Only you may enter. Your warriors are forbidden."

"I understand."

She escorted him into the small room. Tomar expected this room to be larger. No matter, perhaps he could find something useful in here.

"This is the personal records of every ruler of Loma, at least those records that weren't destroyed in the great fire. You may take your time."

"Thank you for your generosity."

"You are most welcome. It's the least I could do after the knowledge you have given to our healers."

"Empress," a young warrior female called out.

"If you will excuse me, I have much to attend today," she said.

Tomar simply nodded his head. He watched her go to the warrior, then that look of shock on her face told him she had found out that Queen Rhaya was gone.

"Search the highlands. That is the only retreat she could have used."

"Yes your highness."

After the females had left Tomar began pouring over the scrolls. It was almost morning when he emerged from the chamber.

"Great Tomar, you look distressed," one of the Rundal guards said as he quickly brought Tomar some water.

"I may have made a mistake introducing the Malka people to the Loma warriors."

"Should we ready the ship?"

"Yes. We will be leaving this afternoon. Don't tell any of the Loma warriors about our plans. Make sure all our warriors are on that ship. We are going home."

"Yes Tomar."

Another warrior brought Tomar some food and more to drink. Tomar sat down and slowly began to eat.

"Tomar what is going on," one of his head warriors said as he sat down at the table.

"I thought I was helping the males of Malka. Maybe I still am. They aren't coming. Hell, maybe the empress forbidding the males from coming was a good thing after all."

"No disrespect, but you aren't making any sense."

"There was no natural disease that killed the male warriors on this planet. It was manufactured. When the first smaller males came through the anomaly they saw it as a sign from their Goddess. The females on this planet had far superior intellect than the males. I don't know…perhaps the first empress didn't want to share power…" Tomar stood. "Maybe they thought they could contain the disease."

"They killed their own males?"

"Yes, two hundred years ago when that anomaly first appeared, they set out to rid themselves of the large male warriors. They murdered so many of them. What am I going to tell Niro? Will he allow those Loma warriors who are already on Malka to stay? Will he kill them all to protect his males?"

"Niro wouldn't do something like that. The way these females talk I don't think they know what happened all those years ago."

"No, they don't, they were fed lies their whole life. No wonder the empress wanted to destroy Queen Rhaya's village just to get to the male child."

"This makes no sense why would they kill off their males?"

"I don't know. I wanted to help these people."

"You didn't know, Tomar."

"I will have to think on what I will say to Niro when we arrive home. I only pray that he doesn't punish those refugees for what a handful of royalty had done. I wonder if Queen Rhaya knew this. The first thing we must do when we arrive home is question her. What if she carries the disease? What if this was the empress' intentions."

"I don't think so. The whole palace is in an uproar over Queen Rhaya being gone. I believe the empress thoroughly intended in destroying that whole village."

"Yeah you're right. We must quickly ready to leave. I believe the empress has no intention on letting us leave."

"Why do you say that?"

"She wouldn't have allowed me to read those scrolls if she intended on allowing us to leave. We have some sort of purpose to her."

"She thinks you were sent by the Goddess."

"I know. I don't really want to know what her intentions are. I just want to get home and make sure Queen Rhaya won't harm the males of Malka."

"I will hurry the warriors. I will come for you when the ship is ready."

"Alright."

Tomar paced through the library. The female leaders of Loma murdered their males. A manufactured disease that targeted testosterone, the more testosterone a person had the deadlier the disease was. Tomar was angry and he felt guilty all at once. Niro was trying so hard to save his people. Natural disease took the females from Malka. What was Niro going to do when he learned what the Loma rulers had done? He heard footsteps entered the library.

"Why?" he said, knowing it was Aviva standing behind him. He could smell her perfume.

"I am assuming you are speaking of the disease."

"Yes."

"The Goddess gave us the knowledge it was her will."

Tomar quickly turned around. "Your rulers twisted the words of your Goddess. My people have learned many terrible and destructive things. Yet, we have chosen the way of peace."

"Surely you who have been sent by the Goddess should understand her ways."

Tomar couldn't say anything further. He couldn't risk Aviva seeing him as anything less than a deity. He had to get his people off of this planet. "You are right. I don't know what I was thinking."

"Now I wish for you to dine with me this evening. I wish to know more about your people."

"I would be honored, though I would like to retire to my chamber until then."

"By all means please do."

Tomar left the library and headed back to his chamber. He needed Sasha's arms around him, needed to hear her voice and feel her warmth. He has put the males of Malka in grave danger. He could only pray that Queen Rhaya was the person he thought she was when he decided to help her and her people escape from Aviva.

Chapter Seven

"Laigne, would you be happy on Loma?" Robin asked as she laid Rose down for a nap.

"Malka is my home." Laigne finished putting away the linens.

"Yeah but on Loma you would be treated better."

"I am happy here with you and the children." Laigne noticed Robin moved stiffly this morning. "Are you injured?"

"Oh...let's just say Niro...well...let's just say he really missed me."

"Oh." He looked away from her. "I know it's not my place, but he should be more careful with you."

"I enjoy it when Niro is a bit rough. He doesn't do anything that doesn't bring me pleasure." She could see Laigne becoming more uncomfortable. "Anyways, I feel sorry for Zenos. He is going to miss Zenith so much."

"Zenith has been his trainer for a couple of years now."

"It's more than that. Zenos is already trying to contain his feelings. My little six year old boy is trying so hard not to let it show when he is hurting."

"All male warriors are trained at a young age not to show feelings."

"It's stupid. Zenos is just a boy. I bet you weren't allowed to show feeling either were you?"

"No one really cared if I showed emotion or not."

"What about your parents?"

Laigne finished putting away the linens then just stood there. "My father sent me away when I was really young. I don't even remember what he or my mother looked like."

"Sent you away. Why? Where?"

"I am a weaker male. It was quite obvious that was what I was going to be when I didn't grow as fast or strong as the other boys. No warrior wants a weaker male for a son. I grew up with the other weaker males. We were taught to do a servant's work and…"

"And what?" Robin gently grabbed his arm.

"To be submissive."

"They groomed you to be a sex toy for the…ahh!" Robin grew angrier by the moment. "This shit is going to stop."

"Please." He turned to her and looked her in the eye. "You are brave for trying to change things. But until there are enough females for the warriors nothing is going to change. I am grateful that I was born in the Dascon clan."

"Grateful."

"If I was born in the Larmat clan I would be dead already."

"This is so unfair."

"It is the way things are."

"Well the way things are…oh it's just stupid." Robin turned to the door when she saw the large male warrior enter. She glanced over at Laigne as he moved from the warrior. His body was tensed up. He was trying to make himself invisible to this warrior. Even though there was no way that warrior would touch Laigne right in front of Robin, Laigne was so use to the way things were he instinctively took a defensive stance. The warrior didn't even acknowledge Laigne's presence.

"What is it?"

"A Loma warrior has request to see you."

"Show her in."

The warrior nodded his head and left the room. Within moments Fenalla entered the room. Her eyes locked onto Laigne.

"Niro's mate, I have a request."

"Please call me Robin. What was your name?"

"I am called Fenalla."

"Fenalla, please tell me what your request is."

"I would like to spend time with your male."

"With Niro?!" Robin said that louder than she intended.

"Oh no, not Niro. I would never touch another female's mate."

"Well that's good to know."

"I want to spend time with Laigne." Fenalla smiled at him.

"Oh…well…" Robin turned to Laigne. "Would you like that Laigne?"

"You wanted me to help you clean today."

"That can wait. Would you like to spend time with Fenalla?"

Laigne looked up at Fenalla. He couldn't deny he liked the way she looked at him. No female ever looked at him like that. Hell, no female except for Robin even acknowledged his existence before. "Yes, I would," he said quietly.

"Please be careful not to leave him alone."

"I will protect him. I give you my word as a warrior."

Robin watched as Fenalla gently grabbed Laigne's hand and led him out of the room.

"What are you looking at?"

"Niro." She leaned back into his embrace as he hugged her from behind. "That Loma warrior wanted to spend time with Laigne." She sighed when Niro cupped her breasts with his hands. "You have about worn me out. You can't possibly..." She gasped when he bent her over so that her hands were touching the bed to hold herself up. "I just put Rose down for a nap. You are going to wake her up."

"Then we will have to be quiet."

Robin heard fabric ripping, but before she could turn around to see what it was Niro place the fabric in her mouth and tied it behind her head, making a crude gag. He squatted down behind her pulled her covering up and started lapping at her pussy.

"I could lick your pussy all day, my female." His greedy tongue hungrily lapped all her pussy and ass. "I want you good and wet." He growled as he stuck his tongue deeply in her.

Robin moaned loudly, but the gagged stifled it. Her body moved around as Niro licked at her. She felt dizzy when orgasm after orgasm ravished her body. She sighed when he wrapped one of his powerful arms around as he drove his fingers deeply into her, he used his thumb to rub her clit while he gently caressed her asshole with his tongue.

"Niro!" she cried out, but it was muffled by the gagged. Her body slumped forward.

"Damn you taste so good," he growled as he stood. He pushed her down onto the bed then climbed on behind her. He lifted her hips and drove his cock hard into her. "Your pussy is so wet...mmm warm....ahh!" he purred. "That's it tighten that pussy up, squeeze my cock." He slapped her ass hard. He reached over and undid the gag.

"Ride me hard, my male, fuck me brutally."

"Rrrrahhh," he growled loudly. He slammed his cock into her causing the bed to lurch forward. He drove his cock so hard and fast he hoped he wasn't hurting her. Yet, he couldn't stop, his orgasm was building and building. He howled as he came then his body collapsed down onto hers.

Robin loved when his large body completely covered hers. It was a little hard to breathe, but it was worth it to be covered like this.

After a couple of moments Robin heard Rose starting to cry.

"Oh no, we woke her up."

Niro rolled off of her.

"And we moved the damn bed across the floor," Robin said as she quickly wrapped herself in her covering.

"Mmm," was the only thing Niro replied.

"Why don't you go comfort your daughter?" Robin playfully punched him.

"I am too sated to move."

Robin hurried over to Rose's room.

ഇഇഇ

Fenalla had Laigne show her around the village of Dascon. She didn't really notice the strange looks from the male warriors. She was with Laigne and that was all that mattered. She dared any of these male warriors to even think about touching Laigne. She was ready and quite able to protect her small male.

"You are quiet," she said when they returned to the leader hut.

"I am not a very interesting person I am afraid."

"Yes you are." She gently grabbed his hand and led him to her chamber.

Laigne looked around her small chamber then he glanced up at her.

"I want you. Will you allow me to take you?"

"What?" He backed up to the door.

"You are so beautiful." She removed her shirt then her pants. "That's it let your eyes caress me."

"Any of the male warriors would be honored to be with you. You should…"

"I don't want them. I want you." She moved closer.

"They would know what to do. I…"

"Shh…" She placed her hand on his mouth. "I will show you." She lifted him up and carried him to the bed. She gently laid him down. "Will you allow me to take you?" She wanted to just ravage him, but after knowing what the smaller males are forced to endure from the large males she couldn't bring herself to just take him.

"Yes," he said quietly.

She quickly removed his clothing then climbed onto the bed. "By the Goddess, you are beautiful," she said, running her hands down his body. "So beautiful." She kissed down his smooth body. "I am going to suck on your glorious cock until you are breathless."

"Ahhmmm," he hissed when she took his cock into her mouth. Her mouth caressed him so expertly. He wondered where she learned such skill.

"Mmm, beautiful male," she purred as she devoured his cock. He tasted so good, his cock felt so good in her mouth, oh damn he smelt so good. She wanted to suck on him for hours.

Laigne reached his hands up and gripped onto the sheets. A most wonderful feeling was starting to build at the very core of his being.

"Damn, my male, oh look at you." She watched him as she continued to suck on him. The pleasure that showed on his face was intoxicating. She slowed her sucking wanting to prolong this ecstasy.

"Please…please…oh please," he begged. He wanted to feel the apex of his pleasure.

"A little longer. I want to see you in pleasure a little longer."

"Please Fenalla." His body arched as his cum filled her mouth. He could feel her hungrily suck up every drop. He couldn't breathe, think, all he could do was feel. His body shuddered from the intensity of his orgasm. He could feel her tongue lapping at his balls as he slowly came down from his pleasure high. He didn't deserve this heaven. He was no warrior. She deserved the strongest most fierce of all warriors to match her skill.

"Stop," he whispered. "I don't deserve this."

Fenalla climbed up his body until she was able to kiss him. She softly kissed him. "I must show you that I deserve you, beautiful male."

"Stop!" He gently tried to push her off of him. "I don't deserve you. No male warrior will want you if they know you have been touched by a weaker male."

"I don't want them. I want you." She sheathed his cock with her pussy. That look on his face was almost too much. Pleasure and sadness mixed in his beautiful dark eyes.

"I want you, Laigne," she repeated over and over as she rode him to nirvana.

She arched her body up as her orgasm overtook her. "Beautiful male," she purred as she looked down into his face. She smiled then climbed off of him. She lay beside him and slowly ran her fingers up and down his chest.

"Did I bring you pleasure?" he asked quietly.

"Oh yes," she cooed.

:"I won't tell anyone about your gift to me. No warrior will ever find out you allowed a weaker male to…"

"I want you, Laigne. How many times do I need to say this? I don't want a barbarian warrior."

Laigne didn't know what to say.

"You don't need to say anything. Just lay here with me."

He snuggled up against her. He tried hard not to let his tears flow. He never even dreamed that a female would want him. He had given up hope of ever having a moment like this.

"I will prove myself to you. I will make myself worthy of you," she said as she held him closer.

Worthy of him, he bit his lip hard to stop his tears from flowing. He wasn't going to cry. Males don't cry, not even a weaker male.

Chapter Eight

"Zenith!" His mother hurried over to him.

"Jena, let the boy catch his breath for a moment," Dalas said.

"Father." Zenith bowed his head in respect to his father.

"You look well," Jena said as she looked him over.

"It's good to see you, Mother." He kissed her softly on the cheek. Zenith looked a lot like his father, though he had his mother's warm smile.

"Ramiro, you are looking well too."

"As are you, Jena."

"The whole village misses your father terribly."

"I am sure he will return soon."

"Your mother arrived safely. She is in her hut."

"I will make sure to stop by and see her."

"More Loma warriors?" Dalas watched the females coming off the ship.

"The older one is Queen Rhaya. This is from Niro." Zenith handed Dalas the note.

"Jena, we are commanded to show this queen the utmost respect and cater to her wishes." Dalas put the note away. "We are also supposed to keep our warriors in check. With so many human females in this village I don't know how Niro expects me to watch them all."

"You must be Dalas," Rhaya said as she approached.

"Yes, I am. How do you wish me to address you?"

"Rhaya is fine."

"My mate will show you to your quarters. I am afraid I have something urgent to attend to or I would have escorted you myself. Please excuse me."

Rhaya nodded her head.

"Please follow me. Zenith go with Ramiro to see Sasha."

"Yes Mother." Zenith couldn't stop himself from gazing at Petra as she passed. That wicked smile on her face instantly brought his body to life.

"Are you going to be her protector?" Ramiro asked.

"Petra's protector?"

"If you are mating with her shouldn't you honor her by becoming her protector?"

"I doubt she wants me to be her mate."

"Do you want to be her mate?"

"I am too young to be a protector. Another male will just take her from me in a challenge."

"I have seen you fight. You are quite good. Why else would Niro allow you to train his son."

"Because I am younger that's why. An older warrior may hurt Zenos."

"You should honor her."

"She doesn't want me anyways."

"Oh, that's why she is always seeking you out. She could easily find warriors to mate with her if this were the only thing she wanted."

"We don't have time for this discussion now."

"That's right run away, like you always do."

"Don't start this. Besides you told me you were curious about a human female and I don't see you going after Mara. It's obvious she wants you."

"We weren't talking about me."

"Uh huh, who's running away now?"

"I told you, it would be frowned upon for a Rundal male to take a human female."

"When did you start caring what everyone thought?"

"Let's go." Ramiro grabbed his bag and headed toward the village.

"Whoa, you Rundal have been busy." Zenith looked around the village. There were lots of new huts being built.

"More offspring are being born and surviving. Our numbers have almost doubled over the last five years."

"I can see that."

"Plus now with the Loma warriors living here we will need to build even more."

Zenith observed the Rundal and barbarian males busy building. It has been awhile since Dascon has grown.

They continued on ahead. The main part of the village was bustling with the day's activities. Zenith smiled seeing so many Rundal hatchlings running around. A Rundal was considered hatchlings until their tails grew long enough to touch the ground, then they were simply called young. Once they choose a mate they were called Rundal. The Rundal liked to keep things simple. Since Ramiro was Tomar's son and assumed more responsibility he was already given the honor of being called Rundal, even though has not chosen a mate.

They headed to the large hut that housed Tomar and Sasha.

"How many brothers and sisters do you have?" Zenith said looking at the group of hatchlings playing. Though he knew him forever, Ramiro never spoke about his family all that much.

"Six, my mother allows the other hatchlings to play in the hut. These two are my sisters," Ramiro rubbed the tops of their head. "Two of my older brothers died when our planet was destroyed. My older sister is now Talk's mate. And my older brother helps my father rule."

"Shouldn't you be helping rule too."

"Alamaxa is the eldest he will be the next ruler."

"Why is it I have never met him before? You would think…"

"He lives in seclusion. Only my father and mother speak to him."

"What about his mate?"

"Of course she lives with him. I believe they even have a hatchling."

"You don't know. Haven't you seen the hatchling?"

"I am not permitted to see Alamaxa. This is the way of my people. When the eldest son is being groomed to be the next leader he immerse himself in the task. I will see Alamaxa when father relinquish control over to him or he needs to step in while father is gone."

"That could be years."

"Then it will be years before I see him."

"Where does that leave you?"

"I will be the grand warrior. I will help Alamaxa with the warriors."

"So you are like Demos."

"Yeah, pretty much."

"Ramiro," Sasha opened her arms to him as she entered the room. Ramiro went over to her and gave her a big hug.

"You look distressed?"

"I am worried about your father."

"You shouldn't worry."

"He is my mate. I can't help but worry about him. Zenith it's good seeing you back in the village."

"It's good to be back."

"Your mother must be so happy. She really misses you when you are away."

Ramiro stepped back when a large Rundal male entered the room.

Zenith instantly went on alert. He didn't like that look on Ramiro's face. "Who is this?" he asked.

"Alamaxa," Ramiro said softly. "Mother what has happened to father?"

"Be calm." Alamaxa's voice was deep and carried much authority. "We are preparing for the unthinkable."

"What has happened to father?"

"We must hope for the best yet prepare for the worse, Ramiro." Sasha went to him.

"You are the grand warrior. Act like it," Alamaxa scolded.

Zenith watched as calm come over Ramiro.

"Mother has told me you haven't chosen a mate. You will do so by month's end."

"Alamaxa…"

"Mother, Ramiro needs to grow up. By month's end you will have a mate either you will choose her, or I will. Do you understand?"

"Yes."

"Hey, you can't speak to him like that. You are not Tomar."

"It's okay." Ramiro grabbed Zenith's arm.

"I have more important things to do," Alamaxa said as he left the room.

"Tomar isn't dead, nor will he be for some time. What gives Alamaxa the right to speak to you that way."

"Be calm young Zenith. This is the way of our people," Sasha said.

"Tomar doesn't act like that."

"Tomar is one in a million." Sasha walked over to Ramiro. "I am afraid it is time for you to choose a mate Ramiro. Alamaxa will choose one for you if you haven't done so by the month's end. He is not like your father."

"Don't worry about me, Mother," Ramiro said in a soft tone. She had enough to worry about. He will deal with this by himself.

"I must tend to Queen Rhaya. Why don't you take Zenith to his chamber."

"Yes Mother."

Ramiro motioned for Zenith to follow him.

"Ramiro…" Zenith didn't know what to say. Now he understood why Ramiro was so moody here lately.

"We will talk later Zenith. You should really get some rest now."

"But…I want to help you…somehow."

"Don't worry about me. I have a whole month to deal with this."

Ramiro bid Zenith goodnight then he headed to his chamber. Alamaxa has always been so much more than him. He is smarter, stronger, larger, hell he even has a bigger presence to him. Most importantly Tomar saw Alamaxa as more.

Ramiro walked into his chamber then headed for the balcony. He liked being in Dascon more than the Rundal village. The barbarians were so uncomplicated. Being the second oldest son to the grand leader of the Rundal people was almost too much. Grand warrior…Ramiro chuckled, the barbarians protected his people. There really was no need for a grand warrior.

Ramiro spotted Mara walking down the path toward the leader hut. She and Petra were escorting Queen Rhaya. His tail twitched side to side as he watched her. She was so focus on her task. His eyes caressed her form. His attention was taken away briefly when he spotted his mother greeting Rhaya. Then quickly his gaze returned to Mara. His breath caught when their gaze met. Her attention went back to her queen as they headed inside.

Ramiro walked away from the balcony and went over to his large bed. He could picture Mara lying in his bed awaiting him. His tail twitched faster as a clicking noise escaped from him. His cock grew harder and harder the more he thought about touching Mara's soft flesh.

He quickly pulled himself out of his fantasy. He didn't dare to think he could actually touch Mara like that.

His attention went to the door when he heard the soft knock. Slowly he opened the door. A female Rundal stood there.

"My name is Ree, Alamaxa has sent me."

He sniffed the air catching a whiff of her arousal. "Come in." His body was heavy with need. He couldn't turn this female away.

Her tail flicked back and forth as she sniffed. She removed her clothing and climbed on the bed. She pushed her tail aside and lifted her ass in the air.

If he took her, he would have to consider her as a mate when time came to choose. Right now, he needed release. He made a fast clicking sound which caused her to purr. He lowered down and sniffed at her pussy. The smell of her arousal was intoxicating. He flicked his long reptilian tongue tasting her nectar. He caressed her tail then used his tongue to lick on the underside of her tail. This made her purr louder. He stood up and grabbed her hips. Slowly he stuck his large cock into her pussy. His tail came up and caressed her as he thrusted slowly. Her tail came around and caressed his ass. He clicked loudly when she took the tip of his tail into her mouth.

"More, take more," he growled. The clicking noise he made became louder and faster letting the female know she was giving him much pleasure. She took as much of his tail into her mouth as she could manage. He stroked the underside of her tail as he thrust faster and faster.

She purred loudly as she orgasmed.

The clicking noise coming from him stopped. He hissed like a snake as he came hard. Slowly he pulled his cock from her. He bent over and used his long tongue to lick at the back of her neck. She sighed with satisfaction.

"I want to be your mate, Ramiro," she purred.

He said nothing as he helped her out of the bed. He wrapped her covering around her. He gently took her hand and kissed it.

"Thank you," he said softly.

She smiled then left the room

"Damn you Alamaxa," he growled. "Damn you to the depths of oblivion." Now he had no choice but to choose a mate. If he didn't Ree would become his mate. Alamaxa would make certain of it. It wasn't fair to Ree or him. He didn't love her, hell he didn't even know her.

He stomped over to his bathing chamber. His body was sated, but his mind was in turmoil.

Chapter Nine

"The little lizards are cute," Mara said as she watched a group of newly walking hatchlings passed by.

"Yeah they are," Petra replied. "Do you think Fenalla has claimed that small male back at the barbarian village?"

"If she hasn't I bet she is really trying."

Mara watched the two female Rundal walk by. Their bodies had a human female shape. "The lizard females are as dainty as the barbarian females."

"I haven't notice, but I guess you are right."

"I wonder if it's okay to look around."

"I see no harm. The queen is resting and the lizard males are guarding her chamber. I wondered where the barbarian males stay when they are stationed here."

"No, you wonder where Zenith is."

"Well...yeah...I need his body."

"Since he is the son of the barbarian general who is stationed here I bet he is staying in the leader hut. Isn't Ramiro the son of Tomar?"

"I think so."

"Then he would be in the leader hut as well."

Petra looked at Mara funny.

"What?"

"You want that lizard male? I thought you were just curious about the lizard male's form, but now I think you really want Ramiro."

"I am curious. He seems like he would be gentle."

"You want to bed a lizard male?"

Mara was silent for a moment.

"Do you?"

"Yes."

"Eeuuu," Petra said as she stood. "Why? There are so many barbarian males. Eeuuuw…a lizard male…oh…that's so gross."

"Stop it!" Mara stood up and glared at Petra. "One of them will hear you."

"I couldn't even imagine…gross."

"Stop it!" Mara shoved Petra back. "I heard the barbarian males bed the female Rundal."

"That's gross too."

Mara gave Petra a dirty look then stomped off.

"Mara wait!"

"Leave me alone. Go find your barbarian and just leave me alone."

Mara walked around the village. She couldn't help what she felt. Ramiro intrigued her. His voice was so gentle. She like the way he carried himself…like a warrior. He was so eloquent and intelligent. He was the son of the leader of the Rundal and yet he didn't act like he was better than any of his comrades.

"Hey female I am talking to you."

Mara turned around and instantly went on guard when she looked up at the large barbarian male.

"What do you want?"

"To feel your pussy sheath my cock."

"That's not going to happen."

"I love the fight you large females have. But in the end I get what I want."

"You have been with other Loma warriors?"

"Oh yes, some willingly some not. It matters little to me."

"You better pray I didn't here you correctly."

Mara looked over at Ramiro as he approached them.

"This doesn't concern you, Rundal."

"I am called Ramiro, son of Tomar, and it does concern me."

"Forgive me I didn't know your station."

"Did I hear you correctly? You have forced yourself on the Loma warriors."

"I have only taken what has been given to me freely."

"Go, but be warned, Alamaxa has decreed that any male that takes a female against her will, will be arrested."

"Who is this Alamaxa?"

"The acting leader of the Rundal. Dalas, the barbarian general has agreed to this as well. Do you understand?"

"Yes." The barbarian stomped off.

"Is this true?"

"Yes, my brother wanted to help Dalas control his warriors. Why are you wandering around by yourself?"

"I am a warrior I can take care of myself. My queen is resting your warriors are guarding her so I know she will be safe. Why are you wandering around?"

"I was heading back to the leader hut after seeing my warriors in their barracks. Would you like to join me?" He knew he should just let her go about her business, but he wanted to be near her.

"Am I allowed in the leader hut?"

"If you are with me it's fine."

"Okay I would like to see the leader hut." Her heart pounded in her chest. She could smell his scent and she liked it. It was delicate with just a hint of male musk. Sweet, yet spicy, it was his own scent not some manufactured ones like the barbarian females wore. Petra's reaction to her wanting to be with Ramiro kept haunting her. Would all of her people have this same reaction? The females were curious about the Rundal. But she wasn't sure it was sexual, like her curiosity.

She followed him to the leader hut. She couldn't stop herself from stealing glances of him. His body looked like a human males, it moved like a human male. She couldn't stop herself from wondering if his cock was the same as a human male's. The texture and color of his skin was different but this only sparked her curiosity more. Her eyes wandered down to his tail. It was slightly twitching side to side. She glanced up at his face. This is where he was very different than a human male. His face had reptilian features mixed with a human males feature. His eyes looked human, he had lips like a man, but that's where the similarities stopped. The rest of his face was reptilian his tongue was long and forked. He didn't move his mouth when he spoke which at first was a bit distracting.

"What is it?" he asked when he noticed her staring at him.

"Can I see your teeth?"

"Why?"

"I am curious."

Ramiro hesitated. His teeth were sharp and pointy and he had almost twice the number of teeth than a human did.

"Please."

"I don't want to frighten you."

"I won't be."

Ramiro stopped walking and looked at her. She was almost the same height he was. He opened his mouth. His tongue instinctively flicked out. It was twice as long as a human male's tongue.

"Wow."

He quickly shut his mouth. "That is why we speak with our minds. We only open our mouths to eat."

"If you bit your enemy you could do some serious damage."

"Why would I bite my enemy?"

"I would if I had teeth like yours. In our training we are taught to use our entire body."

Ramiro just looked at her. She wasn't upset at all. She seemed fascinated by him. He wasn't expecting that reaction.

"What is it?" she asked.

"You are not afraid of me or disgusted by me now?"

"Why would I be? I assumed you had a long tongue, you're reptilian. Your teeth are not scary, just fascinating. I don't understand why you are not trained to use them when you battle. I could never be disgusted by you. Please don't ever think that again."

"I don't know what to say?"

"Then don't say anything." She smiled at him and started walking forward.

He caught up to her and smiled at her. When a Rundal smiled you can see it in their eyes.

He showed her around the leader hut.

"You remember my mother Sasha."

Sasha looked surprised at first but quickly gathered herself. "You are one of the queen's guards."

"Yes, I am called Mara. It is an honor to be in your hut, mate of Tomar."

"Ramiro…"

"I asked her if she would like to see the leader hut."

"If I shouldn't be here I can go."

"No, no, it's alright, please enjoy your stay. I must excuse myself. I have important matters to attend to." She watched Ramiro escort Mara away. She didn't like that look about Ramiro. He was happy like a male would be when he has chosen his mate. Alamaxa would never allow Ramiro to be with a human female, for that matter neither would Tomar. She saw Ramiro place his claw gently in the small of Mara's back as he led her away. Like a Rundal male would do to his mate.

"What's wrong Mother?" Alamaxa's deep voice startled her.

"Nothing."

"Then come back inside. We still have much to discuss."

"Alright. I will be there in a moment."

Her heart ached for Ramiro. Why did he have to fall in love with a human female, especially when there were so many Rundal females who wanted to be his mate? By Rundal standards Ramiro was very attractive. Surely by human standards he must be terribly unattractive. Then why was this human female interested in him. Was it the fact he was Tomar's son. Sasha was going to find this out. Perhaps if she let the human female know that it was Alamaxa not Ramiro who was going to be the next leader, maybe she would lose interest and let Ramiro choose an appropriate Rundal female to be his mate. Sasha headed back into Alamaxa's chamber and resolved to seek out Mara tomorrow.

Ramiro escorted Mara back to where Queen Rhaya was staying. He couldn't stand being that close to her without touching her anymore.

"When can I see you again?" Mara asked when they arrived at her chamber.

"You want to see me again?"

"Of course."

"I don't know…" He was shocked when he felt her soft hand on his face. She gently stroked his small muzzle.

"I want to see you again." Her body started to become aroused. His skin was soft, yet rough, the texture was slightly different than human skin.

"It is forbidden for a Rundal male to mate with a human female." He didn't want to say that but he had to let her know.

"I don't care. Even if we can't be intimate I still want to see you again."

He placed his clawed hand over her soft hands. He didn't know what to say.

"Please let me see you again."

"You have to see me as grotesque."

"No…you are beautiful to me."

Ramiro stepped back.

"Do you see me as grotesque?"

Ramiro looked into her beautiful dark eyes. "No…I think you are more beautiful than the sunset, than the most delicate of flowers…you are beautiful to me."

Tears filled her eyes. Both didn't know what to say or do at this moment.

After a few moments Ramiro gathered himself. "I will come for you tomorrow. I must train with my warriors. Would you like to join me?"

"Yes," she said quietly.

Ramiro walked away. He had to get away from her before his heart burst.

Mara went into her chamber and collapsed on the bed. The tears fell from her eyes. His words touched her profoundly. She was happy and sad. It was forbidden for them to be together. Even her people would frown upon it. They would probably react the way Petra did. But…he had to feel the same way she did or else he wouldn't have bothered to say anything.

Chapter Ten

Robin entered Noland's chamber. She had arranged to speak with him today. He was from Earth and she was most eager to talk to him. Niro didn't mind because he saw Noland as a weaker male.

Noland was sitting in a rocking chair in the middle of the room. He was gazing out the window with his infant son cradled in his arms. He seemed deep in thought. He looked so sad.

"If you would like to be alone I can come back tomorrow."

"I'm sorry I didn't hear you come in." Noland stood and walked over to the cradle that was next to a large bed. He gently laid little Noland in the crib.

"Is he asleep?"

"Yes, finally."

Noland escorted her out onto the balcony. "This planet is very beautiful."

"Yes it is." She stood next to him.

"Tell me do you miss Earth?" he asked.

"Not at all."

"Me either. But..." He gripped the rails of the balcony.

"What's wrong?"

"If I was still on Earth Brian would still be alive."

"I am so sorry."

"That bitch's assassins just killed him and his mate right there, right in front of me and Adrianna. Brian was my best friend and his mate Maya was Adrianna's. She killed them because Maya was pregnant. Adrianna blames herself for having a male child. Can you believe that? My beautiful mate blames herself for Brian and Maya's death."

"The empress won't be able to hurt you two, well you three counting little Noland."

"That bitch wants my son dead. Why?" He looked at her.

"I don't know. I wish I could give you an answer."

"These large men on this planet look at Adrianna funny. I don't like it. I don't really care what they think of me, but she has been through enough."

"Niro will make sure none of his warriors bother her."

"Your mate has been most generous."

Robin could tell Noland was not up to any visitors. He was so sad. She turned around when she heard someone enter the room.

"What has happened?" Adrianna hurried over to them.

"Nothing, I just came to talk with your mate." Robin watched as Adrianna ran her fingers gently through Noland's hair.

"I am sorry. I am being terribly rude," Noland said.

"Don't worry about it. You have a lot to think about. I should be getting back to my chamber. I am sure Rose will be waking up from her nap any time now. When you feel better I would love to talk with you."

"Alright."

Robin left the room.

"She is from your home planet, my male."

"I know. I don't like thinking about Earth too much. I like being with you and there was nothing on Earth I am going to miss."

"But she is Niro's mate. He is the ruler of these people."

"I will talk with her later."

"My male tell me what to do to bring that smile back on your face."

"I miss Brian and I am sure you miss Maya."

"Yes I do."

"I just want to know why the empress had them killed. The medicine people predicted Maya was going to have a girl."

"Do you know what I think?" Adrianna walked back in the room. "I think they were killed by accident. I think we were the target of the assassin's blade."

"Why do you think that?" Noland followed her to the bed.

"Remember I took little Noland to be cleanse in the sacred river. I thought the Goddess could anoint our little child and bring him luck. Remember?"

"Yes, I remember. I also insisted that I was coming with you."

"Brian and Maya were standing in front of our hut as we came back into the village. That is when the assassin attacked. She moved so fast that she had killed both of them before the other warriors managed to kill her."

"No, that can't be. Maya was pregnant. Besides what does it matter. Nothing will bring them back."

"But…they died because of me."

"Don't say that." Noland took her into his arms. "Don't you ever say that. They died because of the empress. She is the only one to blame here. Little Noland was suppose to symbolize that your Goddess had forgiven the males of your planet. This should have been celebrated. Something just isn't right. The truth will come out."

"What if she sends assassins here to hurt little Noland?"

"Then you will kill them. I know you will protect our son." He could see the calm come back to her face.

ཙཪ

"Take it easy," Demos said as he took the sword from Nina's hand.

"I feel fine. I want to finish my training session today."

"No."

"Excuse me."

"I said no. You will go rest."

"Have you lost your mind? Don't try that macho male crap on me…"

"Calm down, female."

"Oh don't even…"

"Nina, please go rest. You look tired. Please, do this for me."

"That's not fair. Oh alright I will stop training. But you can't treat me like a fragile thing. I might end up killing you before I have this baby."

"One of the Rundal will be checking you to make sure you are fine."

"I am just fine. Please stop fussing. This baby…"

"It's you I am more concerned about right now."

"In that case you can relax because I feel just fine."

"You look tired. Nina…" Demos gently grabbed her. "If the Rundal tells me that you will be harm having my child then I would rather not risk…"

"I am having your baby. Robin had two large babies. Sabrina is about to pop out another, hell all the Earth women have had babies, so I think I will be just fine. Please stop worrying."

"Demos," a young warrior hurried over.

"What is it?"

Niro has got a signal from Tomar. He will be arriving in a few days. Niro wants you to come to his chamber."

"I will be there shortly."

"Yes Sir." The warrior hurried off.

"You better get going."

"Not until I have escorted you back to our hut."

"You don't need to…"

"I will carry you to the hut if need be."

"Alright, I will let you win this argument. Let's get going so you can go to Niro. It sounded kind of urgent, judging by how fast that warrior ran out here. When you are done, maybe you can tuck me in." She smiled seductively at him.

"I think it is better if you rest."

"You have barely touched me since you found out I am pregnant. You do know pregnant women can still have sex?"

"Yes, but…I don't want to hurt you."

"I am not going nine months without having that gorgeous body of yours. Hell no. You won't hurt me. We will discuss this later. We better get moving." She laughed loudly when Demos picked her up. "You are going to carry me all the way home aren't you."

"Yes, so you better hold on."

Chapter Eleven

Ramiro walked over to the hut where Mara was staying. He found himself eagerly anticipating seeing her again.

"Ramiro." Mara hurried to him. She was dressed in her training clothes. She had her sword strapped to her back.

"I see you are ready."

"I am eager to train with you." Her eyes caressed him. She took in all of him. He was dressed like the barbarian warriors. She walked behind him and let her hand caress his sword. The large sword he had strapped to his back was beautifully made.

"Who crafted this sword for you?" she asked as her fingers lingered on the blade.

"It was a gift from Niro when I was named General of the Rundal warriors."

"Lead the way."

She followed him through the streets of the Rundal village. She was barely aware of anything else but him. Yet, Petra's reaction from yesterday still haunted her.

They entered the training grounds. There were barbarian warriors training with Rundal males.

"The barbarians have been most generous with helping train the young Rundal males."

"Don't your people have their own form of training?"

"Of course, but most of the grand warriors didn't survive my planet's death."

"I heard about what happen to your people. I'm sorry."

"I was but a small hatchling when it happened." He pulled his sword out. "My two eldest brothers died. They stayed behind to pilot ships. They couldn't clear the blast zone in time. All I remember was seeing my mother cry. That's how I knew my eldest brothers weren't coming back. My father was so strong. He managed to comfort us and our people. Alamaxa has my father's strength. Yet, he doesn't have my father's compassion."

"I have never met this Alamaxa. And I have only spent a short time with the great Tomar. But the few moments I spent with him I could see his greatness. I can see a lot of his greatness in you."

"No...not me, Alamaxa has father's leadership talents."

"You are more than you see yourself as, Ramiro."

Ramiro gazed into her eyes. Her words were genuine.

"Shall we spar?"

Mara pulled her sword out and readied herself.

They trained together for about an hour then Ramiro went over to the young Rundal warriors and started them on their drills.

"Why aren't there any Loma warriors training?" Mara asked while they took a break.

"I have set up a separate training ground for them to use. The barbarian males have a problem with females being on the training grounds. And with the constant sexual tension between the barbarian males and the Loma females no one would get any training done."

"You are very wise." She placed her hand on his upper thigh.

Ramiro quickly stood. He was surprised by her tender touch.

"Ramiro!"

"Mother." Ramiro hurried over to her.

"Your father is on his way home." Her eyes danced with life. "I got his transmission. He said he will be stopping here first before heading over to Dascon." Sasha looked over to Mara. "I must speak with you alone, Ramiro," she said quietly.

"Mara, I will be right back." He motioned to two young Rundal males. "Would you run these two through those drills I showed you?"

"Of course."

Sasha gently grabbed Ramiro's hand and led him over to the other side of the training grounds. She looked around to make sure there were no other Loma warriors around. "Why is that Loma female at this training ground? I thought you had another area set up for the female warriors to train."

"She is with me."

"Why?"

"She wanted to see the training grounds. Now what did you want to tell me."

"Your father wants you to keep an eye on Queen Rhaya."

"Why?"

"He wouldn't get into it. He didn't have much time to speak. He just said it was of the utmost importance that we keep an eye on her and the Loma warriors. Plus, he wanted to know if any of the barbarian males have fallen ill since the Loma warriors have shown up. To my knowledge they haven't. Have you heard anything?"

"No, none of the barbarians are ill. What's going on?"

"Tomar said he will explain everything when he arrives. So I want you to have the Rundal guards keep an eye on Queen Rhaya. To me she doesn't appear to want to cause any harm to anyone."

"How much longer before father will be home?"

"Two days. I haven't told Alamaxa yet. There was no time for your father to speak with him. I think it might be best if we didn't tell Alamaxa anything yet until we know what's going on."

"But Mother…"

"I know what you are going to say. It's protocol to tell Alamaxa everything, but what if he keeps the Loma warriors confine to their huts? They have been through enough. I don't want them to feel unwelcome. I mean what if the barbarians confined us and watched us with suspicious eyes when we first arrived. I doubted that the trust that we have now between our people would have been as strong as it is now."

"I understand what you are saying. I will simply have the Rundal warriors who are guarding Queen Rhaya give me a report about what she did each day. Nothing will seem out of the ordinary that way."

"I will let you get back to training." Sasha turned to leave then stopped. "Ramiro…"

"What is it Mother?"

"You do remember it's forbidden to lay with a human female."

"Of course I do. Why are you reminding me of this?"

Sasha turned around and looked up at him. "That Loma warrior is human. I see the way you look at her and I have noticed she looks at you the same way. You will only get hurt. Tomar will not allow you to mate with a human female."

"Mother…"

"The barbarian males don't have enough females to keep their race alive. It would almost be like spitting in Niro's face if one of our males takes a human female as a mate. Do you understand? There would be no offspring from such a union and one of the precious few human females would be taken from the barbarians."

"I understand Mother," Ramiro said curtly.

She just nodded her head and walked off the training grounds.

"Is everything alright?" Mara said as she hurried over to him.

"Yes everything is fine. I think it's best if I escort you back to your chamber."

"Allow me to make you a meal."

"I don't know…"

"Please, it's the least I can do. Come by the hut this evening. I will put a Loma twist on your native dish using the meat of that creature called a trof. I have been experimenting and would love your opinion on what I have come up with. Please say you will come."

"I would be delighted to join you for dinner."

That smile on her face warmed his heart. He dismissed his warriors and walked her back to her hut. He didn't give her time to touch him. He couldn't handle that right now. He had much to do. He had to make sure his warriors got their new orders.

ഇ ഇ ഇ

Zenith rammed his cock hard and deeper into Petra. He had her pinned facing the wall. He held one of her legs in his arms while his other arm was wrapped tightly around her waist. The fact that he was only four inches taller than her made this position possible.

"Harder, oh damn harder," Petra purred. Her hands pressed harder against the wall.

"Oh, you are going to make me come again…"

"Not yet, wait male wait. Oh yes, yes…like that, oh yes like that."

Zenith bit his lip hard to keep himself from coming. He felt her whole body shudder as she cried out his name. That was it, his control was gone. His orgasm ripped through causing him to howl.

He slowly pulled his cock from her and lowered her leg down. He pressed his body against her keeping her pinned to the wall.

"Mmmm, you know how to use that big cock of yours," she purred.

He nuzzled his face against her soft hair. "Petra..." he whispered as he breathed in the scent of her hair. He stayed like that for a moment then stepped back. He walked over to the bed and sat down.

He let his eyes linger over her strong, beautiful body. The thought of another warrior touching that beautiful body bothered him.

"What's wrong? Did I wear you out?" She chuckled.

"I could never tire of taking your body." He lay back in the bed. He felt her climb onto the bed.

"Then what is it?"

He gazed into her warm brown eyes. "I want to be your protector," he said softly.

"What does that mean?" She sat up.

"I want you to be my mate. By becoming your protector I will prove myself to you. Prove that I can protect you and our offspring."

"I can protect myself and my offspring." She climbed out of the bed.

"Other males will want to claim you as their mate. I will fight them off..."

"Hold up." She looked at him sitting there. He looked so vulnerable at this moment. "You are saying you want me to be your lifemate. Do you love me, Zenith?"

"Yes or otherwise I would have not asked you to allow me to become your protector. Do you love me?"

She couldn't deny she loved having his body. But if sex was the only thing she wanted she could easily have her fill from the other barbarian males. Yet, she sought Zenith out. He was the only male she wanted touching her.

"I have never been in love before. I'm not sure if what I am feeling is…"

Zenith stood and walked over to her. "I have never been in love before either. I find myself thinking about you all the time. When Ramiro told me I should honor you by asking to become your protector all I could think of is what if I can't protect you. What if some other male defeats me and takes you away. What if you didn't want me? When I see you my heart warms, my body comes to life. This must be love that I am feeling. Lust doesn't feel this complete."

"Zenith…" She didn't know what to say. Her heart started to beat faster when he came down to his knees before her.

"Give me the honor of being your protector. Allow me the chance to prove that I am worthy of your love."

Complete…what a perfect word for him to use. "I don't understand your custom, but if this allows me to be your mate then yes, I want you to be my protector."

She was surprised when he leapt up to his feet and grabbed her. He threw her on the bed then grabbed her hips lifting them in the air. She gasped when he shoved his cock deeply into her. He thrust wildly as he bent over pinning her to the bed. He bit her shoulder and growled as he thrust harder and harder.

"You are my female," he growled as he bit harder. "I am your male, tell me, say it," he growled loudly.

"You are my male. You are my male!" she cried out.

He howled like an animal as his cum filled her then his body collapsed down onto her.

"I will prove I am worthy of you. I swear it," he whispered into her ear.

She didn't say anything. She lay there enjoying the heat of his body as he covered her.

Chapter Twelve

Ramiro wanted to cancel his dinner with Mara. For that brief moment when she asked him to dinner he forgot he was a Rundal. A Rundal usually doesn't eat in front of the barbarians, only during special ceremonies will they do so. When a Rundal eats it's strange looking to the barbarians. Those barbarians that live here were use to it.

"Ramiro, there you are." Zenith hurried over to him.

"Hey Zenith you look happy."

"I asked Petra to allow me to be her protector and she said yes."

"That's great news. What made you decide to go ahead and ask her?"

"I couldn't stand the thought of another male touching her. I think I love her."

"You think?"

"I have never been in love before. I have been in lust many times, but never love."

"I am happy for you Zenith. I am sure you will prove yourself worthy of her."

"I heard Tomar is coming back."

"Mother is excited."

"What's wrong?"

Ramiro looked at Zenith. If there was one person he could completely trust it would be Zenith. "Mara has asked me to dine with her and I said yes."

"Okay, what's wrong with that?"

"I'm Rundal remember. My dining habits will probably frighten her."

"Oh…well just explain to her before you start eating."

"I don't know. I think it's best that I just cancel our dinner. Besides, mother has a couple of Rundal guards following me now."

"What? Why?"

"She is very adamant about me not seeing Mara."

"You are just having dinner with Mara. I see nothing wrong with that."

"Mother sees plenty wrong with that. She luckily hasn't told Alamaxa yet. I am sure she is waiting to tell father."

"Maybe she has told Alamaxa."

"Trust me if she did Mara would be confined to her chamber or I would be. Alamaxa keeps sending Ree to my chamber at night."

"Who is Ree?"

"I am guessing my intended Rundal mate. I can't help but take her when she enters my chamber. I am a male and she wants me. She is a very beautiful female."

"But…you want Mara."

"I want her with all my being, Zenith. I can't stop thinking about her. Every time I get near her my body demands hers. Yet, I can't touch her. But it's more than that. I love the sound of her voice, that smile on her face, the way she looks at me. I could just sit there and stare at her for hours. Just being near her I feel…right, you know what I mean."

"Yes."

"Mother sees what I feel for Mara that's why those two guards over there have been following me around all day."

"You can't help who your heart wants."

"Mother said if I take Mara as a mate it would be like spitting in Niro's face. I have too much respect for your people to take one of the few precious female humans away. Tell me honestly, would you be angry at me if I was to take Mara as a mate?"

"You are my best friend. If she makes you happy I wouldn't be angry at all."

"But the other male barbarians would be."

"Honestly…yeah they probably would be. And they would demand you follow our custom of being Mara's protector first and prove yourself worthy of a female."

"It's best that I just leave Mara alone. I will tell her tonight."

"I think it's best you step up your training and prepare to be her protector."

Ramiro looked at Zenith for a moment. "I couldn't fight a barbarian male."

"Sure you could. I have seen you fight. Hell, my father helped train you so you know how a barbarian fights."

"There is no way my father would approve of me taking Mara as a mate."

"As long as you take her in our custom I see nothing wrong with it. Are you that afraid of your father?"

"I don't fear my father. I respect him. What about my people. They will not approve of this either."

"Then it's best if you leave Mara to a male who is willing to fight for her."

"What?!"

"It sounds to me that you are afraid to fight for her."

"I am not afraid."

"Then prove it."

"I can't take Mara as a mate. It's wrong."

"Then the least you can do is tell her tonight."

"You're right. I better prepare. Thank you for listening."

"You have listened to me countless times. I have to get back to Petra. I have announced that I am her protector.

So far no one has challenged me. Niro has told my father to only allow about ten of the Loma females to be chosen as mates. He wants to be able to spread the rest out amongst the other males in Malka. He is even going to let the Larmat males choose a couple of them."

"How do the Loma females feel about this?"

"Queen Rhaya has agreed to these terms. My father can't believe that five of the Loma warriors will have weaker males as mates. Can you believe that?"

"Yeah, but a weaker male wouldn't be able to fight off challengers."

"They won't have to. This is the bargain Niro made with Rhaya."

"It's only five females."

"Five too many in my opinion. Weaker males will only produce weaker offspring and they haven't trained or are able to defend their mates."

"You really don't like weaker males do you."

"No, they simply accept their fate. I would rather die fighting than be some large warrior's plaything or someone's servant. If I was curse with being born as they were I would still train. I would fight for the right to do so. I would prove myself worthy. Yet, those pathetic weaker males just take whatever happens to them. When I was twelve summers old I came back from training. I had never seen a weaker male before. As you know I have lived in Rundal pretty much my whole life. My father took me to Dascon with him this time. I was so honored being able to train with the warriors who lived in Dascon. Anyways, on the way back I saw this really small male. He was busy cleaning something. I was curious about a weaker male so I was going to go talk with him. This large warrior walked over to the weaker male and grabbed him. He pushed the weaker male to his knees and forced him to suck his cock. That weaker male didn't even fight he simply sucked on the large warrior's cock. It made me sick to my stomach. There was no way I would allow another male to do that to me. When the warrior was done he pushed the weaker male to the floor and walked off. All that weaker male did was huddle in the corner. No anger, no nothing. Since then I have no use or respect for any weaker male."

"Perhaps that weaker male did fight in the beginning and it did him no good. You large warriors are very strong. Maybe fighting only makes things worse for that weaker male. To me he was doing what he must to survive. There is no punishment when a warrior kills a weaker male is there?"

"There didn't use to be. But Niro's mate Robin has changed that."

"I am glad to hear that. A weaker male is still human, Zenith. Tell me, would you look down on a female if she didn't fight off a male warrior?"

"Of course not, that is what her protector is for."

"A weaker male is lacking in strength just like a female. The only difference is that they have no one to protect them. So at least five of those weaker males will have a Loma warrior to protect them. Something for you to think about."

"You better get ready. You don't want to keep Mara waiting."

"You're right."

Ramiro went to his chamber. He had so many thoughts going through his head. He cleaned himself and put on a fresh loincloth. He could barely remember what the male Rundal use to wear on their home planet. The weather was so warm on Malka it was more practical to wear the loincloth. The female Rundal dressed like the barbarian females with slight alterations to accommodate for their tails.

He went over to Mara's hut. He could smell the delightful aroma of the trof meat cooking.

"You're here."

He was surprised when Mara hurried out of her hut toward him. That look of excitement in her eyes enthralled him.

"I have forgotten to tell you something."

"You can tell me inside." Mara led him into the hut. "There are two Rundal males following you."

"I know. You are very observant."

"I am a Loma warrior. Why are they following you?"

"To report my comings and goings to my mother."

"Why would she…"

"Let's not discuss that. Dinner smells wonderful."

"I have used some of the spices from my planet. I wanted to use some of the fruit but what we have brought have to be tested to make sure it is compatible with the local crops."

"I must tell you something about how a Rundal eats."

"Okay."

"It's well, kind of gross to a human, I guess. That's how some of the barbarian males have described it."

"It matters little to me. You can't help how you eat."

"My father is careful when he dines in front of any human. But this takes years of practice."

"It's okay. Don't worry about it. Sit down. I will serve up dinner now. You have to eat this food warm."

Ramiro moved his tail out of the way as he sat down. He was so nervous. He didn't want her to see him as gross or worse that he may frighten her.

She set the plate of food in front of him then sat across the table with her plate of food. "Eat. Tell me what you think." She started to eat.

Ramiro paused. "I can't. I don't want to frighten you."

"It won't. Now please eat. I can turn around if you wish."

"That's okay. That would be rude of me to make you feel uncomfortable."

Oh, that smile on her face. It warmed him so. It was best if she saw everything about him. Perhaps she would be so disgusted she wouldn't want to see him again. It would be the best thing for her. A human male would be more suited for her. Yet, his heart ached thinking about never seeing her again.

He cut up the meat into big pieces then his tongue flicked out and grabbed a piece of it. His mouth slowly opened revealing his many sharp teeth. He had to leave his mouth open as he chewed or otherwise he would bite his long tongue. The chewing, ripping noise as he tore and chewed the meat with his teeth was rather loud. When he finished with the first piece he looked at Mara. She seemed unaffected by his eating habit.

"Well, do you like it?" she asked.

"It's very good. The spices are very delicate."

"All the people in the village learn to cook. It's part of our training."

"Really?"

"Oh yes, all people in the village learn many skills. It makes the village more productive."

"The Rundal learn many skills too, especially the hatchlings and the young. Once you learn what you are really good at you then teach it to the next generation. The Rundal believe in the tribe, not just the individual families."

"It's the same with the Loma. When males were plentiful each village was like a tribe, all working for each other. I have noticed the barbarians seem to focus on family units. Except for Niro. It is apparent that he loves his family, but he thinks of his people as well."

"They believe in the clan. I don't know what you mean."

"The weaker males, they care little about them. If we were on Loma weaker females are not treated differently and are not considered worthless. They are part of the tribe and are treated as such."

"Oh…I haven't seen a weaker female. You all look to be well trained."

"Because we all train. If you look out amongst the people of my village you will see the smaller females. Those big male warriors have already claimed most of them as mates. Petra is the only stronger female with a protector so far. Of course Niro has said only a certain number of females may be given to the male warriors here. I believe that number has been reached. So out of the females allotted for the warriors here all the weaker females have been chosen."

"Petra is the only strong warrior chosen?"

"Yes. The others will have to wait for mates when Niro sends them to the other villages."

"It's strange that I didn't notice the smaller females."

"Why?"

Ramiro looked at her when he sensed the hint of sadness in her voice. "Nothing really, it's just that I am usually so observant. I will have to make sure to practice more on that skill."

"Oh…"

He could see the smile come back to her eyes.

They finished dinner.

"I hope I didn't disgust you too much."

"Not at all. I figure that Rundal would eat differently than us. To be honest some of those male barbarians eating habits are worse. They talk with their mouth full, they tear off chunks of meat and spill food and drink all over themselves. If I can stomach that I can pretty much take anything."

Ramiro chuckled. "I better go."

"No, please stay." She moved closer to him.

"I can't."

"Please stay." She reached her hand up and timidly touched his chest.

"Mara, it is forbidden for us to be together."

"I don't care." She pressed her body against his. "I want to be with you."

"I can't be your mate. I don't want to dishonor you."

"I want to be with you." She looked up into his eyes. She didn't care what everyone thought. She wanted to feel him, taste him…love him.

His tail twitched back and forth. A clicking sound escaped from him before he could stop it.

"Why are you making that noise?"

"I am aroused."

His tail twitched faster.

"Then you do want me. I am yours, take me. I want you to take me."

She stepped back and removed her covering. The clicking sounds coming from him grew louder. This strangely excited her more. She watched as he removed his loincloth. Her eyes devoured his cock. He looked just like a human male.

"I don't know how to start," he said.

She moved closer as she reached out her hand and grabbed his large cock. The texture was slightly different than a human male's cock. The clicking sounds grew louder and faster from him as his tail thumped the ground. She slowly came down to her knees. She took his cock into her mouth. She had to taste him. His cock wasn't smooth as a human male's was, yet it was still soft to the touch. He tasted so good. Slowly she slid his cock in and out of her mouth, sucking and licking every inch of it. She kneaded his balls in her hands as she sucked. The skin covering his balls was very soft and smooth. She could hear his tail thump the ground and that clicking noise become faster until it almost sound like he was purring.

She was startled when his tail began caressing her. He quickly stopped.

"Don't stop," she said, looking up into his face. His tongue flickered out as he leaned his head back. His tail caressed her body tenderly as she went back to sucking his cock. The top of his tail was the same texture of his cock but the underside was very soft. It felt wonderful being caressed by it.

"I want to feel your mouth on my cock all night, but if you don't stop I will come. I don't want to come yet." He gently helped her up to her feet then lifted her up into his arms. He carried her to the bed and laid her down.

His hands wandered over her body. The silky softness of her skin was intoxicating. He used his tail to flick at her clit as he ran his fingers over her nipples. He looked into her face when she moaned loudly. He lowered himself down letting his long tongue taste her skin. His tail explored her body as his tongue tasted the sweetness of her pussy.

"This is almost too much," she purred. She could feel his long tongue snake over her pussy, flicking and rolling covering every inch of her pussy. His tail caressed her breasts; his hands massaged her inner thighs as his tongue tasted her.

Her body trembled from the intensity of her orgasm. She grabbed his tail and gently stroked the underside. He lifted his head from between her thighs and hissed. She took the tip of his tail into her mouth and started to suck on it, watching his reaction. She grew more excited seeing that look of pleasure dancing across his face. She used her hands to stroke up his tail as she continued to suck on it.

"I need to take you now." He climbed on the bed and position himself between her legs. He slowly filled her with his cock.

"Oh my Goddess," she cried out. His large cock completely filled her, but it was the rough yet soft texture of his cock that was so heavenly. She could feel every inch of him go in and out. She never felt such a feeling. She had one of the barbarian males when they first arrived; her body demanded that she let the male take her. His cock felt wonderful, but not like Ramiro's cock did now. The texture felt amazing, that coupled with how his tail felt and tasted. She was in nirvana

"More…take more…" his voice wavered. He hissed loudly when she took more of his tail into her mouth. The clicking sound intensified when she stroked higher up his tail. .

"Goddess, sweet Goddess!!" she cried when she orgasmed again. She stroked his tail like she would have his cock. She quivered when his long tongue flickered across her face. So many sensations going on at once, she was almost purring from the pleasure of it.

"Mara," he growled when she took his tail back into her mouth. His orgasm began its slow ascent. He couldn't breathe as his orgasm slowly built and built. He quicken his thrust wanting his orgasm to crescendo, but it kept building, bringing him so much pleasure he could barely stand it.

"Ramiro," she purred as her tongue flickered across the underside of his tail.

"Ahhhsss!!!" he hissed loudly as his orgasm finally exploded. His cum pumped into her until he thought he might die from the pleasure of it. He collapsed down onto the bed. Half of his body covered hers. He couldn't move after such a powerful orgasm. No Rundal female ever brought him to such heights of pleasure before.

"Are you okay?" Mara asked as she caressed his back.

"I will be."

"That was amazing," she said as she kissed up his arm.

"That don't even begin to describe the nirvana you have given me."

He felt her hand travel up his tail. He might die if she touched his most erogenous zone. He held his breath anticipating her touch. She managed to sit up as her hand traveled higher up his tail.

"Ohssmm," he purred when she caressed the underside of the base of his tail.

He felt her leave the bed as she continued to caress the right spot.

"Don't," he quickly said when she began licking that same spot.

Her hand went to his cock and started to gently stroke his now hardening cock. She licked feverishly at the base of his tail.

"Too much pleasure...Mara...I am going to...ohhhhh!!!" His orgasm slammed him so hard his body trembled. No Rundal female every tasted him right there. "Mara please stop...I can't take...anymore."

Mara climbed back into bed. "Your skin is so soft right in that one spot. It's softer than a human female's skin."

"It's the most sensitive spot on a Rundal male."

"What about your females?"

"The back of their neck is their most sensitive spot." He sat up and pulled her to him. He moved her hair out of the way and let his tongue flicker over the back of her neck.

"Ramiro," she purred. Her whole body tingled as he licked the back of her neck.

His tail came around and caressed her pussy.

"I can use my tail to fill you. Would you like that?" he whispered in her ear.

"Yes."

His tail snaked into her pussy, slowly inch-by-inch his tail filled her. He went as deep as she could take then slowly moved his tail in and out, in and out, as he licked at the back of her neck. His hands came up and kneaded her breasts as he continued to fuck her with his tail. The softness and wetness of her pussy felt so good on his tail. His cock started to grow hard again.

"Ramiro…oh Ramiro," she purred as her first orgasm ripped through her.

"I can take you like this as long as you want."

He used his tail on her for an hour until she just couldn't take anymore. He rolled her over, so he could take her from behind. Slowly he let his cock fill her.

"Take your pleasure Ramiro. I…" She was breathless.

He rode her hard and fast letting his orgasm come quickly then he lay on the bed beside her. "I can use my tail again if you need more."

"No…" She snuggled up beside him. "I think I just might die from pleasure if we do anymore. I just want to hold you now."

"That sounds good."

He liked how her body felt against his. Loved the sound of her soft breathing and the way her hair felt like silk against his skin.

"Ramiro…"

"What is it?" He stroked her hair.

"I love you. I want to be with you like this forever. You don't have to say anything. I just wanted to let you know that I love you."

"Mara." He nuzzled his muzzle against the top of her hair. "I love you, but we can't be together. Now I fear that I will bring you only pain. I should have never…"

"Shh, it was worth any pain that I will feel later. I will find a way for us to be together. I will speak with my queen."

"Mara, no."

"I will Ramiro." She looked up into his face. "I want to be your mate. I don't care whether your people, the barbarians or my people like it or not."

He didn't know what to say. He just pulled her closer and held her tightly to him.

Chapter Thirteen

Fenalla waited impatiently to see Niro. She wasn't sure of the barbarian custom of claiming a mate. She thought about talking to Robin, but Niro was the barbarian's leader.

"Niro will see you now. Don't waste too much of his time," the very large male warrior said as he glared down at her.

"I don't care whether you like me or not. So glare at me all you want."

The large male smiled at her. "I might have to ask Niro to be your protector. I would love to dominate you, strong one."

"Just show me to Niro."

She walked into Niro's chamber. Demos was talking with him. She looked around hoping to see Robin. To her relief Robin was busy with Rose. Her heart pounded hard when she spotted Laigne helping Robin.

"What do you want female?"

Her attention quickly went back to Niro.

"I have come to ask your permission to be someone's mate and protector."

"Tell me what warrior has got caught eye?"

"Warrior?"

"What warrior do you wish to be your protector?"

"I don't want a warrior. I am a warrior."

She quickly looked over to the door when Nina entered.

"Demos, I have seen the Rundal healer and he said everything is alright. He also said as long as I am careful I can still train."

"I don't know if I want you to train while you are with child."

"I should have a say in this shouldn't I? We will discuss this later. Oh, I am sorry did I interrupt something."

"This female wants to choose a mate. Tell me who have you chosen."

"Laigne."

A hush fell over the room.

"What?" Robin walked over to them.

Fenalla ignored them all and went over to Laigne. She came down to her knees before him. "I want to be your mate, Laigne. I am unsure of the barbarian custom, but it is the custom of my people for the female to claim the male. I swear I am strong enough to protect you and I will spend my life making you happy."

"He is a weaker male," Niro said as he stood.

"Niro…" Robin gently grabbed his arm.

"I have given the five weaker males to the female warriors as per my agreement with Queen Rhaya. I will not waste one more female on a weaker male."

"I want Laigne. I will not be a mate to one of your warriors."

"I am afraid you have no choice."

"Niro," Robin said softly as she gently pulled on his arm. "Laigne, do you want Fenalla as your mate?"

"Niro just said…"

"That is not what I asked you."

"You better answer her, weaker male," Niro growled.

"Yes," he said quietly.

Fenalla stood and gently caressed Laigne's face. "Then my choice has been made. I will be Laigne's mate."

"No you won't. I will not waste another precious female on a weaker male."

"Niro…"

"Robin, I have made my decision."

"Niro, please…I want Laigne to be happy. Please let her choose him as her mate."

"Robin," Niro softly said.

"You heard what Niro has decided, female." Demos stood.

"Demos don't you even get involved with this. Can't you see those two love each other," Nina said.

"Demos, it's alright. For my female, I will give you a chance to claim Laigne as your mate."

"Thank you, Niro." Robin snuggled up against his arm.

"What do I have to do?"

"You will become his protector. Since no male will challenge you for him. They will be challenging for the right to your mate. If you are successful then you may have Laigne for a mate. If you are not, then you become the mate to the male who has defeated you."

"Niro that isn't fair," Robin said.

"I agree to your terms," Fenalla said.

"No Fenalla. I don't want you to get hurt," Laigne said.

"No male warrior will defeat me. Not now, especially not now. I have you waiting to be my mate. Nothing will stop me from becoming your mate."

"Then we have an agreement. I hope you are a warrior of your word and if you lose you will still be a good mate to your male."

"You have my word as a Loma warrior."

"Alright, Laigne can stay with you until you are defeated. You have two weeks to fight off the male warriors. I will let my warriors know what's going on."

"Thank you, Niro." Fenalla gently grabbed Laigne's hand and led him out of the room.

"There is no way she will defeat all the male warriors that want her as a mate. The thought of conquering their female will send many warriors over to challenge her," Demos said.

"I know." Niro sat back down.

"You knew she doesn't stand a chance. How could you do that to Laigne."

"You may feel for that weaker male, but I have no such feelings. Five of those females are already wasted on those weaker males. I can't just sit by and see yet another be wasted."

"What about love, Niro. Couldn't you see that Laigne is in love with her?"

"Yeah, you big jerk," Nina added.

"Quiet female," Demos rumbled. "Niro is doing what's best for our people."

"Don't you ever tell me to be quiet again." Nina glared at him.

Demos stood and pulled Nina to him. "We are leaving now."

"What in the hell has gotten into you."

Demos gently lifted her up and carried her from the room.

"You better put me down or I will kick your ass."

Demos sat her down. "Niro, is my ruler. His word his law and yet he gives into Robin constantly."

"Well if you're mad at her take it out on her."

"I am sorry, Nina. You're right."

"Damn straight I'm right. Robin loves Laigne like a brother. She wants him to be happy. You would think after all the help Laigne has given to Robin over the years Niro would at least show the smallest amount of gratitude and let Laigne have a mate."

"Niro is thinking about his people."

"Well, what if Laigne and Fenalla have a female child. Chances are pretty darn good that they will, seeing how pretty much all of Loma is female. Chances are that female child will grow up to be like her mother. Then let's say when that female grows up she falls in love with a male warrior…do you see what I am getting at."

"There are so many male warriors who will never have a mate. Males who have trained to protect their females, offspring and their village. These males have risk their lives protecting their people and yet they will never know the warmth of a female's touch. I can't show empathy toward a weaker male. To me they have not earned the right to have a female."

Nina let out a deep breath. She could see where Demos was coming from. He can't help how he was raised. "On Earth anyone can have the hope of finding love."

"On Earth the males and females are almost equal in numbers. They are free to find love, but not on Malka. Niro has to give his warriors hope that more females will be found. Who wants to live life knowing that they will never know love."

"Alright I see your point. And I am sorry for yelling at you in front of Niro."

"I shouldn't have told you to be quiet."

She wrapped her arms around Demos.

"Now let me take you back to our chamber. You look tired."

"Alright. I am a bit tired."

෨෨෨

"You can't fight off all those males," Laigne said as they entered her chamber.

"I will. Nothing is going to stop me from being your mate."

"I don't want you to get hurt."

Fenalla walked over to him. "You are worth any risk, Laigne."

"No I'm not."

She lifted him up and pinned him to the wall. "Yes you are." She softly kissed him.

"Please put me down."

She did as he asked.

He timidly reached out his hand and begun untying her shirt. She quickly removed her clothes for him. He came down to his knees and buried his face in her pussy. She lifted one leg up and placed it on the bed giving him complete access to her. Her hands gently caressed his head as he lapped at her pussy. She closed her eyes and let the sensations fill her.

"That feels so good."

Laigne licked up every drop of her nectar that dripped from her pussy. He wasn't sure if he was doing this right. He knew how to suck cock, but he wasn't sure how to pleasure a female orally. He felt her lightly pull on his hair directing his mouth higher. He allowed her to guide him. He licked feverishly on her clit. Her hand tightened in his hair holding him where he was.

"Yes, oh yes," she moaned. She could feel every stroke of his tongue. "Like that, just like that." Her orgasm started to build. "Don't stop, please don't stop." She pushed his face closer as she climaxed. She held him to her as her pussy pulsated. Slowly she released him.

She lay down on the bed and opened her legs wide. "Take me, my male."

He removed his clothes then climbed on the bed and slowly filled her with his cock. He thrust in a slow steady pace, thoroughly enjoying the sensation.

"Come, my male. Fill me with your seed."

Her pussy clamped down around his cock which caused him to come hard. Her pussy milked his cock of every last drop of cum. She rolled him over so now she was on top. She loved seeing him under her like this.

"Laigne, I can't wait to you are my mate," she purred.

He just smiled at her. He didn't want to think about anything else right at this moment.

Chapter Fourteen

Tomar hurried down the ramp toward Sasha's open arms. He wrapped his arms tightly around her. "I have missed you so much," he said softly.

"Not as much as I have missed you."

They held each other for a moment not saying anything.

"More Loma warriors?" Sasha said as she saw the fifty women coming down the ramp.

"They helped me escape Loma. I had to bring them with us or else the empress would have killed them."

"What happened?" She stepped back and examined him for injuries.

"I am uninjured." Tomar looked at the twenty Rundal females who were waiting at the end of the ramp. "Please forgive me, my love, but I must go do something."

Tomar headed down the ramp. He instructed two of his warriors to escort the Loma females to where the others were, then he walked to one of the awaiting Rundal females.

Sasha didn't like that look on Tomar's face.

Tomar got down on one knee in front of the female. "I am so sorry. Markly has gone on to the other world."

"What?!" The female started to tremble.

"He died protecting me. I am in indebted to you and your hatchlings. I will provide for you and will find a suitable protector for you."

The female wept openly. Sasha hurried over to her and tried to console her.

"No, Markly!" the female screamed when she saw four Rundal warriors carrying the covered body of a Rundal male. The woman hurried over to them.

"Tomar." Sasha came down to her knees beside him.

"The empress found out that I was fleeing. She sent her warriors to stop me. Ten Loma warriors and one Rundal warrior died. Five of those Loma warriors died protecting me." Tomar slowly got up. "We can't go back to Loma again." Tomar watched the weeping Rundal female follow the warriors carrying her mate's body. "Markly used his body as a shield to protect me."

"His mate will be provided for. What about the death rites?"

"They were preformed on the ship. His soul is at peace. I only brought the body back for his female to have closure."

"Father."

"Alamaxa."

"What has happened?"

"I will tell you everything. But first I must find Queen Rhaya. Tell me, my son, has any barbarian males taken ill since I have been gone."

"None that I am aware of."

"Father!" Ramiro hurried over to him and hugged him tightly. "I am so glad you made it back safely. I saw the body of the fallen warrior."

"Ramiro." Tomar hugged his younger son.

"My guards inform me that a human female stayed in your chamber last night, Ramiro," Alamaxa grumbled.

"Your guards, I thought they were mother's guards."

"No, I sent the guards. Now explain yourself."

"What is going on?" Tomar stepped back from Ramiro.

"Ramiro has mated with a human female."

"Ramiro!" Tomar said. "You know that is forbidden."

"Don't worry Father I will deal with Ramiro. You go speak to Queen Rhaya."

"Don't you dare tell father what to do. He is still the leader of our people," Ramiro growled.

"Alright enough of this, I will worry about this later. I must see Queen Rhaya now. Ramiro summon about six guards right now."

Ramiro did what Tomar asked. He told Ramiro to go back to his chamber and wait for him.

Tomar burst inside Queen Rhaya's chamber. Petra and Mara instantly came on guard.

"It is alright," Rhaya said as she motioned them to sit down. "Great Tomar what is wrong?"

"Did you know? Tell me did you know about the disease?"

"Disease? What are you talking about?"

"Send your guards away."

Rhaya motioned for Petra and Mara to wait outside. Tomar did the same for his guards.

"What are you talking about?"

"Tell me what you know about the disease that killed your strong males."

"It was a punishment from the Goddess."

"Do you swear on your honor that what you are saying is the truth?"

"Of course I do, because it is the truth."

"Then why was it so important that I stay on Loma, so damn important that your empress was willing to kill me and my warriors over."

"I don't know what you are talking about."

"The library for the empress, you are telling me you have never read the scrolls in this library?"

"I am not an empress. I wouldn't be allowed to read the sacred scrolls."

Tomar sat back in his chair.

"What is going on?"

"Your empress allowed me to read the sacred scrolls…" Tomar stood quickly. "That's it. The fire…."

"The great fire?"

"It destroyed the empress' castle didn't it?"

"Many years ago."

"Oh… I am such a fool."

"Great Tomar you are not making sense."

Tomar sat back down. "I am going to tell you something you are going to find hard to believe. I have no choice but to tell you so that you will understand Niro's reaction to this news. That disease your Goddess sent down wasn't the judgment of your Goddess. It was made by one of your healers. When the great illness swept across Loma it was by order of an earlier empress. She saw the smaller males coming through the anomaly as a sign from your Goddess that all larger males should die. She was wrong. Your Goddess would not have wanted her people to suffer like that."

"This can't be true. I was taught that the Goddess wanted to punish the males for their blood lust."

"You were told a lie. When the great fire happened the formula for this disease was destroyed. Your empress must have wanted me to recreate the formula. She had no intention of letting me leave Loma."

"You don't lie, do you?"

"I wouldn't make this up."

"That is why you stormed in here. You were afraid that I may carry this disease with me and I would hurt the barbarian males."

"I am glad you're not."

"You are going to tell Niro aren't you?"

"I have to. I have to explain to him why I can't bring anymore females from Loma here."

"He will kill my people to protect his warriors."

"No, I don't think so."

"How do you know he won't? He must protect his people."

"He won't judge you for what your empress has done."

"Then he will kill me, so he can rule over my people."

"No, I can't see him doing that."

"I need time to think. The empress of the past murdered our males. Why?"

"I am not sure."

"So many years of loneliness. Praying, hoping for a miracle to come from the Goddess something that would save my people from extinction. The females on this planet died from a natural disease. Niro is trying so hard to save his people. They have a Goddess too. Did you know that? Not a God, but a Goddess. I wonder if it is the same Goddess."

Tomar reached over and gently took her hand. She was in shock. It was to be expected after learning such an awful thing about her people's past.

"Niro is going to kill me. I just pray he spares my people. They knew nothing about this."

"Neither did you."

She quickly looked up into his face. "You have to test us to make sure we don't carry any part of that disease. I would never forgive myself if the barbarian males fell ill because of us."

"Alright I will test your blood."

"Let's do it now."

They headed to Tomar's healing chamber. He drew some blood and began testing it. The process took several hours. There was nothing out of the ordinary about her blood.

"Thank the Goddess," Rhaya said. "I want to see Niro."

"I think it might be best if I were to speak with him first."

"No, I will be there when you tell him. Let him take his anger out on me. Perhaps then he will spare my people."

Tomar looked at her in awe. This woman should have been the empress. She truly loved her people. She reminded him so much of Niro.

"Alright, we leave in the morning."

"I ask that none of my warriors come with us. I trust your warriors to protect me."

Tomar nodded his head. He had her escorted back to her chamber then he went back to his. He stepped out on his balcony and gazed out over the Rundal village. He spotted several barbarian males helping Rundal males building new huts.

"Tomar," Sasha quietly said as she gently caressed his back.

"Ever since we landed on this planet the barbarians of the Dascon clan have aided us. They give us so much freely. I can't stop thinking what if Queen Rhaya had carried that disease with her. Sasha, the rulers of Loma manufactured that disease that killed their males. A strange disease that seemed to attack testosterone, a very complex disease that those females made to murder their males. All because the earlier rulers believed that is what their Goddess wanted because of that damn anomaly. What if that disease had come to Malka? All these barbarian males would have died. Niro's people would have ceased to exist all because of me."

"How could you have possibly known that the Loma people made that disease."

"I was so excited about finding females for the barbarians that I rushed into this."

"Tomar, Niro's people are running out of time. They have to produce more offspring. You only did what you did out of your love of the Dascon people. Stop being so hard on yourself. Thank goodness, Rhaya didn't carry that disease. We should be grateful for that."

"I must speak with Niro and tell him what has happen. I hope he can forgive me for my rashness."

"Niro will not think ill of you. He admires and respects you."

"I am tired. I want to rest before I go. I will deal with Ramiro when I get back. Tell Alamaxa not to do anything until I return."

"I will, my love, you just rest. I will wake you when the ship is ready to head to Dascon."

Tomar caressed her cheek. "I am glad to see you think no less of me."

"Nothing will ever make me think less of you. You are a great male. And I am proud to be your mate. Now rest."

He watched her walk out. Just being near her soothed him. He was relieved that Rhaya didn't know anything about the disease. But at the same time he was still beating himself over his mistake.

Chapter Fifteen

Zenith watched Petra train. He loved to watch her. Her strong body moved with such grace. No male warrior could ever move like that.

"Zenith, I challenge you for your female," a deep voice boomed.

Zenith quickly came up to his feet. It was a very large warrior who was at least thirty summers old. Zenith had seen this warrior train, he was very skilled.

Petra hurried over. "What's going on?"

"I am challenging your protector, strong one."

"Zenith?"

"Step back Petra. I must defeat him or I will lose you to him."

"Wait, I want you as my mate."

"The strongest males get to have a female. Now please step back so I can focus."

"Let's go, young one." The large warrior charged at Zenith.

Zenith quickly dodged the sword blow.

"Petra, step back and let your male fight," Mara said as she grabbed Petra's arm.

"What's going on?" Ramiro drew his sword.

"That large male is challenging Zenith. Ramiro stop them," Petra said.

"I can't this is a barbarian custom. Zenith is very skilled he will try his best to protect you from that male."

Mara glanced over at Ramiro. She could see in his eyes that he was worried about Zenith.

Zenith managed to dodge another sword blow from the large warrior. He couldn't keep this up. He had to attack. He charged at the warrior and found himself on the ground. He quickly moved just before the warrior pinned him.

"Damn it," he grumbled. He couldn't lose. He wanted Petra as his mate. No other female would do, he wanted her. He imagined her in the arms of this large warrior. This ignited his anger. He blocked the warrior's sword with his own. He could feel his arms getting tired. This match was dragging on too long. It was now or never. He used his legs to sweep the other warrior's legs out from under him. He moved quicker than he thought he could and pinned the warrior to the ground. He placed his sword to the warrior's neck.

"You are the better warrior," the large warrior grumbled.

"You fought well." Zenith jumped off the warrior and helped him to his feet. The warrior left.

"You were amazing," Petra said as she hurried over to him.

"I almost got myself pinned. I have to be more careful."

"You won, my male that is all that matters. Your custom is strange. On Loma once a female claims a male he is hers."

"I have almost two weeks left to prove that I am worthy to have a female. With your beauty there will be more challengers."

"I knew you could fight off an older warrior," Ramiro said as he handed Zenith some water.

"I was lucky this time." Zenith drank the water. He looked over at Mara then back at Ramiro. "Well, are you her protector?"

"You know I can't be."

"You should be."

"Ramiro," a Rundal warrior hurried over to him.

"Tomar wishes to see you."

"Alright I will be right there."

"Tomar is back?" Zenith asked.

"Yeah, I must go." Ramiro hurried off.

Zenith glanced over to Mara. Anyone could see that she was in love with Ramiro. He looked over at the group of barbarian warriors who were at the training grounds. They were talking amongst themselves. He could see that Mara was their topic of discussion.

"Petra, I have to talk to you about something."

"Mara, would you excuse us?"

"Sure, I will go check on the queen."

Zenith waited for Mara to leave. "I have heard from my father that Mara will be heading to the Dascon village."

"Why?"

"She has been chosen to become a mate for a male from the village of Dascon. The strongest of warriors are being decided now."

"What if she doesn't what to go to Dascon?"

"It doesn't matter what she wants. This is an agreement between your queen and Niro."

"I fear that she has fallen in love with the lizard male Ramiro. Perhaps it would be better if she was chosen by a barbarian male soon. She can't be a mate to a lizard…I mean Rundal male."

"Ramiro is in love with her too. I can see it. Shouldn't they be together?"

"Mara a mate to a Rundal male…no, that isn't right. In fact that is gross."

"I am surprised at your response. I would think you would want your friend to be happy."

"I do want her to be happy. If she becomes a mate to a Rundal, she will be ostracized by my people, your people and the Rundal people. Why would I want to see her go through that."

"Well, I want Ramiro to be happy and if a human female makes him happy then that's who I would want him to be with."

"This is moot anyways. Tomar wouldn't allow Ramiro to choose a human female. But I thank you for telling me about Mara going to Dascon. I will tell her that way she can be prepared."

"Zenith, your father wishes to speak with you," a barbarian warrior shouted out.

"I will see you back in our chamber later. Be careful around these males."

"You don't have to worry about me."

Zenith smiled at her then headed off the training grounds. She watched him run off. She loved the way his long braided hair moved side to side as he ran. Her body was on fire from watching him battle that more experienced warrior. She wished they had time to make love right now. But him being the son of the General of the Rundal village these interruptions were bound to happen. Besides, she better go find Mara and tell her about what Zenith told her. She couldn't stop thinking about all the delicious things she was going to do to Zenith's body this evening.

"Oh damn, this is going to be a long day," she sighed as she hurried off the training ground.

၈၁၈၁၈၁

"It is forbidden!" Tomar raised his voice. Something he rarely did.

"I don't care. I love her."

"Ppfffh, you lust after her. Once your curiosity is sated she will no longer hold your attention."

"Don't say that. I love her. I don't care that she is human."

"You won't have any offspring."

"That doesn't matter."

"It matters to the barbarians." Tomar stood and pushed the table away from him. He began to pace. He had to quiet his anger. He has been debating this issue with his son all afternoon and he wasn't getting anywhere. Ramiro has always taken a liking to the humans. He played with Zenith more than he did the other Rundal hatchlings when they were younger. Come to think of it Tomar rarely saw Ramiro with other Rundal. He mostly spent his time with the barbarians.

"Father, I respect you beyond words to describe, but shouldn't the choice of my mate be mine."

"You are ashamed of being a Rundal aren't you?"

"What makes you say that? I am proud to be a Rundal warrior, damn proud that you named me General of our warriors."

"I never see you with other Rundal. You are always with Zenith."

"I prefer training with the barbarians because they are more skilled at warfare. I train my warriors."

"Yes, but do you have a friendship with any of them."

"I don't like having many friends. Zenith is all I need."

"Once Zenith is joined with his female, she will take a lot of his time. Then what will you do."

"I can be by myself, Father. I will have my own mate by then as well."

"Yes, you will. Alamaxa has chosen Ree as your mate. You will ask her tomorrow to join with you."

"No Father!" Ramiro pounded hard on the table. "I don't love Ree. Hell, I don't even know her that well."

"You mated with her. I would say you know her pretty damn well."

"I took her body, but I know nothing of her heart or mind. It's not fair to her."

"She wants to be your mate."

"She is just saying that to appease Alamaxa. Who would deny their future leader."

"It has been decided. You will…"

"No I won't. I want Mara to be my mate!"

"I forbid this. Mara is going to be sent to Dascon to be chosen as a mate to one of the barbarian males."

"She wants me as a mate."

"She is curious."

"Ask her. Bring her in here and ask her."

Tomar went to the door and motion to one of his guards. Then he slammed the door and headed straight to Ramiro. "The barbarians need every one of their females. We have more than enough females why take one of their females."

"I love her, Father."

"Great Tomar," Mara timidly said as she entered.

"Tell me something and I ask that you tell me the truth. Do you love my son?"

"With all my heart."

"It is forbidden for my people to be with a human. Did he tell you this?"

"Yes, he did."

"And yet you allowed him to be with you anyways."

"I love him."

Tomar walked away from Ramiro and just stood there looking out the window. "What shall I tell Niro? Should I tell him that my people now wish to start taking some of the few precious human females from his males. Tell me Ramiro, what shall I say to him:"

"I will tell him that I love Mara. I will shoulder anything Niro does."

"What about you Mara. What shall we tell your queen?"

"I will tell her."

"You love her, Ramiro. Then why do you wish to see her shunned by the Rundal, barbarians and her own people? I could never do that to your mother." Tomar turned and looked at him.

Ramiro stood there silently for moment. "I don't wish to see her hurt."

"Then you will choose Ree as your mate."

"Ramiro, I don't care what others say." Mara hurried over to his side. "I will endure anything to have the honor of being your mate. But if you love this Ree, then I would want you to be with her. I want to see you happy. I don't care what it cost me as long as you are happy that is all that matters."

"Mara…" Ramiro reached up his claw and gently ran it down her hair. "Father, I choose Mara as my mate. I will abide by whatever custom you and Niro decide I should follow."

"And if Niro decides you should follow the barbarian custom of becoming her protector you will abide by that?"

"Yes Father."

"Mara, you will not have offspring. Are you willing to give that up to be with my son?"

"Yes."

"Then you will go to Dascon with me tomorrow. You two will not be together until after I have spoken with Niro. Mara go back to your queen. Ramiro stay here."

Tomar waited for Mara to leave.

"Your mother has told you what I found out on Loma hasn't she?"

"Yes Father."

"So you know that Niro will be angry with us."

"I know."

"I will not protect you from Niro's anger."

"I understand."

"Ramiro...you are as near to perfect as a Rundal male can be. You not having offspring is such a waste."

"Tell me something Father. If mother was herself, but she was human, would you not be her mate simply because she was human."

"I love your mother with all my heart."

"But would you love her less if she was human?"

"No, I wouldn't."

"I can't tell my heart who to love. I wish I could, but I can't."

"If you have to become her protector, you may not be able to fight off the barbarian males."

"I may not be able to, but I will try with all my skill. I saw Zenith fight off a warrior that had far more experience than he did. By all rights that warrior should have defeated him. Yet, Zenith was the victor. I think his desire to be with the female he loves gave him that extra strength he needed. If he can do this I can surely give it my best to protect Mara."

"Go rest, we leave first light tomorrow."

"Yes Father."

Tomar sat down on the chair. His mind was numb at the moment. He heard the door open and was relieved to see Sasha.

She walked over behind him and started rubbing his shoulder.

"I knew this was going to happen, Ramiro and that human female. We can't tell him who to love."

"He would have made such strong hatchlings for a Rundal female. He has all the strength and intellect of Alamaxa, but he has your heart."

"No, my male, he has your compassion. I would have loved to seen his hatchlings, but I wish to see my son happy more."

"I somehow knew you would say that."

"I was upset at first, but...do you see how he lights up when she enters the room?"

"Yeah, I saw that."

"He loves that human female. If I thought for a moment it was just lust I would insist you forbid him not to mate with that female. But it's not lust it's love. I can see it in their eyes."

"I want you to come with me to Dascon."

"I will be by your side when you speak with Niro. I think you are worrying too much. Niro won't be angry with you. I don't think he could ever be angry with you."

"I hope you are right."

"Now just close your eyes and relax."

"Mmm, your hands can do wonders, female."

Chapter Sixteen

"You have been very quiet," Zenith said to Ramiro as they exited the ship.

"I have to speak with Niro and I am a bit nervous."

"You are going to be Mara's protector aren't you?"

"Yes."

"You are going to be what?!" Petra glared up at Ramiro. "How could you do that to Mara?"

"What's wrong?" Zenith tried to take Petra into his arms but she refused to let him hold her.

"Mara will be shunned. I suppose it matters little to you, after all you are the son of the great Tomar, no one would dare speak ill of you."

"I will protect Mara from harm."

"How? You can't even give her offspring. On Loma being able to have offspring was one of our greatest joys. Especially since only a few of us had mates. You will be taking that away from her."

"That's enough Petra." Mara went to Ramiro's side. "I thought you were my friend."

"I am that's why I am speaking up now."

"Petra…" Zenith ran his hand down her back.

"He is your friend Zenith so you can't see this with clear eyes."

"I do see with clear eyes. I can see that they love each other."

"See Ramiro, it has already started," Tomar said as he walked up to him. Petra and Mara bowed their heads to him.

"Tomar, as always it's an honor to have you in Dascon."

The sound of Niro's voice caught everyone's attention.

"Niro," Tomar said quietly. He was hoping that it was going to be Demos who greeted him at the ship. It would have given him a bit more time to think about what to say. "We have much to discuss. Robin, it is good to see you and your offspring." Tomar looked down at Zenos and Rose.

"Zenith!" Zenos hurried over to him. He was about to hug him then he drew back and gave a warrior's salute.

"Hey little warrior." Zenith saluted him back. "You have been practicing haven't you?"

"Yes. I can show you if you like."

"Zenith why don't you take Zenos to the training grounds, he has been most eager to show you how much he has been training."

"Yes Niro. Come Petra."

Petra bowed her head at Niro then followed Zenith and Zenos.

"I am glad Zenith has managed to hold on to his female," Niro said.

"So am I," Robin added. "Please let's go back to our hut. Queen Rhaya, I am glad you came back to Dascon."

"I am sorry I was delayed. I was curious about how this ship moves and the Rundal pilot was most generous to show me. Niro, me and Tomar need to discuss something with you."

"Let's go then. We will talk at my hut."

Tomar was quiet as they went back to the leader hut. So was Rhaya. This made Niro very uncomfortable. Whatever they had to tell him wasn't going to be good.

As they headed into the hut Tomar turned to Ramiro. "Wait my son until this afternoon to speak with Niro."

"Yes Father." Ramiro followed the other Rundal males to the training grounds.

Just before Mara was about to follow him Sasha gently grabbed her arm. "Your queen may need you, please stay."

"Of course."

Sasha looked over the large human female. She wanted to like her, but she couldn't stop herself from blaming her for Ramiro not choosing a Rundal female.

Mara could feel Sasha's distain for her. She decided it was better not to say anything.

Niro sat down at one of the chairs that were around the large table. He motioned for the others to be seated.

"What is it that you need to tell me?"

Niro listened as Tomar explain everything. He was shocked at first then disappointed. The only Loma females for his males were already here and there would be no more coming. He did have another fifty of them for his males to become protectors of this was at least some hope.

"I am sorry Niro. I should have…"

Niro raised his hand to silence Tomar. "Don't ever apologize to me. After everything you have done for my people I could never show anger or disappointment in you. If it wasn't for you Robin wouldn't have survived her childbirth. Hell, I wouldn't be alive now. I owe you much. Whatever you want it is yours. You need to only ask. But please don't ever fear my anger. I will never have that feeling toward you."

Niro looked over to Queen Rhaya. He didn't know what to think about her. She looked sincere in what she told him.

"I will pay for what my people could have done to your people and great Tomar. I will spend my lifetime making up for what my empress has done to you."

"You have done nothing to my people," Niro said. "I can't fault a village leader with what their clan leader has done. But I do insist that your warriors get tested to make sure they don't carry the disease."

"I have already tested the females in the Rundal village. They don't carry the disease."

"Do you know why the empress who created this disease wanted to murder the males?"

"The only thing I can reason is that she believed that their Goddess wanted this to happen. Nothing else makes any sense. Maybe the empress was insane, who knows."

"The current empress wanted you to recreate this disease?"

"I believe she wanted it on hand just in case you decided to invade Loma."

"The empress hated males," Rhaya added.

"What do you mean?" Niro asked.

"She only had females around her. She didn't want a male mate. She never had any offspring. The commander of the royal warriors is going to be the next empress when our old empress goes on the great journey."

"She had female lovers?" Tomar asked.

"A lot of Loma females had female lovers. With so few males it is to be expected. However, the empress only wanted to be with females."

"I will continue looking for a planet that has compatible females for your people Niro."

"What about Earth? Perhaps a couple of females can still be taken from there."

"Yes, we can continue to do this."

"My males need some kind of hope."

"I understand. There is another matter that needs to be discussed." Tomar motioned to one of the Rundal males.

Within a couple of minutes Ramiro entered the room.

"Go ahead my son."

"Niro…" Ramiro moved closer.

"Out with it. I don't like it when someone isn't forth right with me."

"I want to claim Mara as my mate. I will abide by whatever customs you decide."

"What?!" Rhaya blurted out. "You can't mean, my Mara."

"Yes, the Loma warrior named Mara."

Rhaya looked over at Mara. "Is this true?"

"Yes, my Queen. I wish to be Ramiro's mate."

"This is unnatural. There would be no offspring with such a union."

"Tomar, did Ramiro discuss this with you?" Niro asked.

"Yes, I am against it, but he insisted that he wants no other as a mate."

Niro looked at Robin. She was in just as much shock as he was. He didn't see that coming.

"Do you love her , Ramiro?" Robin asked.

"Very much so."

"And you Mara?"

"I love him."

Robin looked at Niro. She didn't know what to think.

"Ramiro and Mara leave us. I will let you know what I decide."

"No, great Niro, you can't allow this union," Rhaya said.

"Tomar, are offspring possible?"

"No, your males couldn't impregnate our females, so it is doubtful that a Rundal male could impregnate a human female."

"Your males mate with the Rundal females?" Rhaya asked.

"Tomar has been generous with allowing my males to ease their needs with the Rundal females."

"No offence Tomar, but why would a human want to bed a Rundal."

"I can't deny Ramiro his request. Tomar you have allowed my males to be with your females. However, to appease my warriors Ramiro would have to follow our custom of being Mara's protector. I don't wish to see Ramiro get hurt, but he will have to fight to keep her as a mate."

"This is acceptable. If he fails then he will mate with Ree, the Rundal female that Alamaxa has chosen for him."

"Agreed. Rhaya, do you agree with this arrangement?"

Rhaya regarded Niro for a moment. He was treating her like the ruler she was. "I agree."

"Alright then it's settled. Speaking of Alamaxa when do you wish for me to start meeting with him?"

"As soon as it is possible."

"You are not thinking about stepping down as Rundal ruler are you?" Robin asked.

"Yes, I am. I want to focus on my healing and exploring the heavens. Alamaxa is ready to take over for me. I will of course make sure that he can work with Niro and once Niro feels Alamaxa is ready then I will step down as ruler."

Ramiro and Mara entered the room.

"It has been decided that you will follow the customs of my people. You will become her protector. If you can fight off the warriors who challenge you for her then she can be your mate. However, if you fail then Mara will become the mate to the male that defeated you and you will take Ree as your mate."

"I agree to the terms."

"Since you are the son of Tomar you will only have this week to be a protector. The other warriors have already gone through a week. I wish for you to stay in Dascon until the joining ceremony is over. You may leave."

"Your warriors will defeat him." Tomar said as he watched Ramiro leave with Mara.

"Perhaps, but your son is very skilled. He stands a good chance of keeping Mara as a mate."

"Then it's in the Goddess' hands now."

ಐಐಐ

"See, I told you I have been practicing," Zenos said as he put his practice sword away.

"You have done a fine job."

Zenith quickly drew his sword when he heard the sound of a sword being unsheathed.

"Young one, I challenge you for your mate."

Petra grabbed Zenos' hand and led him a safe distance away.

"Zenith will win," Zenos said as he gripped Petra's hand tightly. "That other warrior is called Balasa. He trains with daddy."

"Does he give your father a challenge?"

"Yes." Zenos looked up at Petra when she squeezed his hand tighter. "Don't worry Zenith will protect you. I will help to protect you."

Petra looked down at Zenos and smiled, especially when he drew his sword and readied himself.

It seemed like the battle dragged on forever. Petra couldn't watch anymore and closed her eyes. Zenith was fighting so hard, but he was wearing himself out, probably just like the older warrior wanted him to.

"Yes!!" Zenos squealed.

Petra quickly opened her eyes and saw Zenith standing above the other warrior with his sword to the warrior's neck.

"I told you Zenith would win. Come on." He dragged Petra over to Zenith.

Zenith helped the other warrior up then went over to Petra. He was completely exhausted.

"You did it! You were so skilled," Zenos said excitedly.

"Was there any doubt," Zenith said winded.

"Zenos, come here."

"Daddy, did you see Zenith, did you?" Zenos ran over to Niro.

"Yes, I did. You go to your mother."

"But Daddy, I want to…"

"I said go."

"Yes Sir." Zenos hurried off the training grounds to the awaiting male warrior who was going to escort him to Robin.

"You were lucky, Zenith. Why did you allow him to lead you like that? He was trying to tire you out. I thought you were trained better."

"He won, didn't he?" Petra added, then she quickly bowed her head when she realized who she was talking to.

"Yes he did win, but now he is exhausted. Tell me what are you going to do if another warrior challenges you right now."

"I will defeat him and the warrior after him and so on, if need be. No one is going to take Petra from me."

"You are a very young warrior. A lot more experience warriors will challenge you."

"I know."

"So you can't wear yourself out like that. Watch." Niro pulled his sword out. "When a warrior is waiting, he wants you to strike. If all he does is block and dodge, it's not that he fears your attacks he is just trying to wear you out. It takes more energy to strike than it does to block. Since you are a younger warrior the older one is pretty certain you will be on the attack. Don't let yourself be baited like this. Now charge at me."

Zenith did and he found himself on the ground with Niro pinning him down.

"See, you are too tired to fight. If any other warrior was out on this field you would have lost your mate. Now go rest. And next time be the defender some of the time, not just the attacker."

"Thank you, Niro."

Niro watched Petra and Zenith leave.

"That young one is going to lose his mate," Demos said as he walked up to Niro.

"Yeah, if he keeps going like that. He is so lucky that there weren't any other warriors out here training right now."

"You have much to think about don't you?"

"Tomar just told me there will be no more females coming from Loma. Ramiro wants a human female as a mate."

"I heard. Many warriors are not happy about this. He will be challenged."

"By some, others won't out of respect for Tomar. Now, I called you out here to spar with me."

Niro charged at Demos and they started to spar. He didn't want to think right now. He only wanted to fight.

Chapter Seventeen

"Oh yes, oh sweet female," Laigne purred as Fenalla sucked on his cock. She had pinned him to the wall then went to her knees. She has been slowly sucking on him for awhile.

"That's it, my male, that's the look I wanted to see." She took his cock back in her mouth and sped up her sucking. She could feel him trying to thrust forward. His soft moans drove her crazy. She could stay like this forever. She loved the way his cock filled her mouth, loved the taste of him, and loved the sweet noises he made.

She had managed to fight off two male warriors so far this week. No one was taking her from Laigne.

Her gaze locked on his face as his cum splashed in her mouth. God, he was so beautiful. She slowly stood up her eyes still glued to his face. She stroked his hair.

"That was for the pleasure you gave me earlier." She smiled at him.

He quickly got dressed. "I have to help Robin with the weaker males. Would you like to come with me?"

"Of course."

She let him lead the way.

When the entered the large chamber Fenalla thought she had died and gone to paradise. The whole room was full of small pretty males.

"Hello Fenalla," Robin said.

"Where have all these males been?"

"They are usually in the weaker male hut. But once a month I bring them here so they can rest and relax. Laigne has been helping me with this since I started this up a couple years ago. They all have two days a month where they don't need to fear being used by the large male warriors. Plus, the Rundal train some in the art of healing, others learn blacksmithing and other skills from the generous barbarian males."

"These males are beautiful."

"To you, but the Dascon females don't see them that way. Plus, a male has to fight for his female and there is no way these males could defeat the warriors."

"You are training them. If they are only used as servants and toys why bother."

"Eventually I hope to change the way weaker males are viewed on this planet."

"Your mate is the grand ruler and yet you go against his traditions. Doesn't he get angry about this?"

"Niro knows this makes me happy, so he allows me to do this, though he sees it as a waste of time. I don't expect to change the way Niro's people think overnight, but if I keep trying maybe things will change."

"I hope so."

They spent all day with the weaker males. Fenalla enjoyed watching Laigne helping Robin. She had gained much respect for Robin today. After they were finish they headed out to the training grounds.

"Niro is training with that big warrior Demos," Fenalla said as she took out her sword.

"He has been out here all day. Tomar must have given him some grim news," Laigne said.

"I will have to find out what's going on. I will ask Petra or Mara."

"Female, I challenge you."

Fenalla turned to the sound of the deep voice. It was the same large warrior from when she asked Niro if she could be Laigne's mate. "You," she growled.

"I'm glad to see you remember me. I am going to defeat you female and when you are my mate I will tame you."

"We shall see. Laigne step back."

"Phff, weaker male," the male warrior growled at Laigne.

"Stay away from him."

"I don't give a shit about him. It's you I want. But I tell you what." He motioned to another large warrior. "When I have defeated you I will have my friend rape your weaker male. Let you see what a weaker male was meant for."

Both of the large warriors started to laugh.

"He lays one finger on Laigne and I will kill him."

"What fire you have. I will enjoy taming you."

He charged at her.

"Niro, that female warrior is being challenge by Dake. There is no way she will win," Demos said as he wiped the sweat from his face.

"Good, Dake will make her a suitable mate. Let's take a break and watch them. The match shouldn't take too long. Besides I better make sure Selsa doesn't touch the weaker male, it would upset Robin."

Niro and Demos walked over. Selsa stepped back from Laigne and stood by Niro.

Laigne didn't care how many male warriors showed up. He couldn't worry about them now. He was concerned Fenalla was going to get hurt. She was fighting so hard. Dake was very skilled, could she win against him?

Fenalla fought well, but Dake was far stronger and more experienced than her. He pinned her to the ground. He squeezed her wrist until she dropped her sword. He grabbed it and threw it off to the side. It landed a few feet from Laigne.

"I have beaten you, female. You are my mate now."

"Get off me."

"I can't wait to claim you." He licked his lips seductively.

"Get off her."

Dake looked up then started laughing hard seeing Laigne holding onto Fenalla's sword. "Are you challenging me, weaker male?"

"Yes."

"Laigne no, he will hurt you."

"I challenge you Dake for Fenalla."

Dake stood up and walked over to Laigne. "This should be amusing."

"Niro, can a weaker male challenge a warrior?" Demos asked.

"I don't see why not. You trained this weaker male to be a sparring partner for Nina, let's see what he can do."

"He will probably drop his sword after Dake's first strike. Then he will drop to his knees and ready himself to suck cock," Selsa said.

Laigne prepared himself. He wasn't going to let Fenalla be a mate to this crude male. This warrior didn't love Fenalla, he only wanted to toy with her.

"Prepare to die, weaker male."

"Stop talking and start fighting."

Dake charged at Laigne.

"He can block good," Niro said.

"Yeah, but I never trained him to attack," Demos added.

"Then this should be a short battle."

Niro watched Laigne fight hard. Never had he seen a weaker male fight like this. Laigne was fighting for Fenalla, not for himself.

Dake knocked Laigne down then kicked him hard.

"Stop that!" Fenalla yelled. She was about to charge him when Niro stopped her.

"Leave them be."

"Great Niro, Laigne is going to get hurt."

Niro watched Laigne get up each time Dake knocked him down. It was clear that Laigne was in pain and was starting to become exhausted. Dake pinned Laigne under him.

"It's over, weaker male. It was fun toying with you though. Now be a good little male and go suck off Selsa while I take my female."

"Let him up," Niro said.

Dake quickly climbed off Laigne. He was surprised when Niro walked over and offered Laigne a hand.

"Good fight," Niro said to Laigne.

Laigne grabbed Niro's hand and allowed him to help him up.

"Why are you wasting words on a weaker male?" Dake asked.

"He fought well. You should have been the one to say so."

"He is but a weaker male."

"Fenalla, you may take Laigne as your mate."

"What?! I won her."

"Dake, I will allow you to choose a mate from the other Loma warriors. Do not question me again."

"Please forgive me, Niro." Even though Dake was angry he couldn't say anything to his leader. Niro would take it as a challenge and kill him.

Dake and Selsa stomped off the training grounds.

"Thank you, great Niro." Fenalla hurried to him and bowed her head.

"Call me Niro. I don't like the great part, it makes me uncomfortable. Now go, take your mate. You will be part of the joining ceremony."

"Thank you," Laigne quietly said.

"Now go."

Demos watched them leave. "Did you do that to make Robin happy?"

"No, that weaker male actually fought for what he wanted. He was afraid, he was out matched and yet he took up a sword and fought for her. Now, isn't Tomar examining Nina today?"

"Yeah, I better hurry over there." Demos sprinted off of the training grounds.

He hurried over to the healers ward and straight to where Tomar was. He was puzzled by the strange look on Nina's face.

"What's going on?"

"Ah, Demos, you are just in time," Tomar said as he finished washing his hands. "It seems as though you are having a daughter and a son."

"What? A child can't be both."

"No, not with the Malka people. Your mate is having two babies."

"But Sasha only felt the one life spark."

"Sasha felt a strong life spark. Twins are rare and she had little experience detecting the unique life spark given off by twins."

"Two babies," Demos said as he gently placed his hands on Nina's belly.

"Isn't this great," Nina said as she placed her hand on his.

"Wait, if carrying one Malka baby is hard on an Earth female won't two be dangerous."

"Nature finds a way. I am sure the babies will be smaller. But I will continue to monitor Nina's progress. I will leave you two alone to enjoy your news."

"Two babies, you big lug, that will show those dumb ass warriors of yours. Twins are very rare to your people."

Demos bent over and kissed her belly. "I am too happy for words. But I am worried about you."

"My body is strong, so don't worry. Of course I will look like a blimp by the fifth month probably."

"Blimp?"

"Never mind. I will look like a big fat trof by my fifth month and you will think I am ugly."

"I could never think that. I don't care if you get fat. You are my female, you will always be beautiful to me."

"You are so sweet and the cool thing is you don't even try, you are just that way."

Demos smiled at her. "I will have to add on to our hut."

"Yep, that will keep you busy."

"Promise me you will take it easy. When Tomar tells you to stop training that you will. Promise me."

"I will do what Tomar tells me. Speaking of Tomar, he wants to run a couple more test so I will be here awhile."

"It doesn't matter, I will stay with you."

"Tell me what's going on with the joining ceremony. Has everyone managed to hold onto their mates?"

"So far. Ramiro wants to mate with one of those Loma females."

"Okay, I can't even mentally picture that one. It seems like he would want a Rundal female."

"I would think so. But love is blind."

"That's true."

"Niro surprised me today. That female warrior who was defending herself, well she lost to Dake. Her weaker male took up a sword and challenged Dake. He fought hard but he lost, yet Niro still allowed the weaker male to keep his mate."

"Good for Niro. Laigne has been such a help to Robin, he deserves some happiness."

"I think Niro allowed it because the weaker male stood up for himself. Hell, Niro even treated the weaker male like a warrior by helping him up and telling him that he fought well."

"Well, by the sounds of it Laigne did fight well."

"Yeah, he did."

"Of course he did, you trained him."

Tomar came back into the room. "I have two more tests to run. So far everything looks good."

"That's good to hear," Demos said.

"Tomar may I ask you something," Nina said.

"Of course."

"Does it bother you that Ramiro wants a human mate?"

"Yes, it does, but he seems to really love the female."

"That's so cool that you are allowing him to go through with this."

"He must prove himself worthy to the male barbarians."

"He will. I have seen him train. He fights well."

"Now I need you to lie back."

Tomar didn't want to think about Ramiro right now. He wanted to lose himself in his work. If the Goddess wishes for Ramiro to have a female mate then it will be so.

Chapter Eighteen

Ramiro made a purring sound as his tongue danced across the back of Mara's neck. They had just made love and he was feeling so sated.

"Ramiro..." Mara snuggled closer to him. She loved the way his strange skin felt against hers, the heat of his body and that wonderful clicking, purring noise he made.

"What's wrong? Did I not satisfy you?"

"Oh Goddess knows you satisfied me, so much so that I can't move a muscle."

"Then what's wrong?"

"I am worried about you. What if one of those barbarian males hurt you? What if your people can't accept me and make you pay somehow? What if..."

"Shhh, all of that doesn't matter. Right here, being able to lie next to you like this, is the only thing that matters, though...I don't want you to give up your chance to have offspring by becoming my mate."

"I was thinking about that. I remember something one of the barbarian females told me. She said that the Larmat clan kills the weaker males. If they deem a male infant not large enough, or if he is oddly shaped they will kill the infant. No weaker male survives past the age of four summers old in the Larmat clan. Although now that a barbarian named Alistair rules the Larmat people this practice is frowned upon. It still happens in the smaller villages. I was thinking that maybe we could take in a couple of these offspring and raise them. And perhaps any Rundal offspring who lost their parents we could take them as well. I know we can't take all of these offspring in, but maybe four or so. Of course if this is alright with you."

Ramiro rolled her over so he could look in her eyes. "That is a wonderful idea." He smiled at her with his eyes. A Rundal's eyes lit up when they smiled.

"I am glad you like my idea."

"I can't wait until you are my mate."

He was surprised when she reached up and pulled him closer. Her soft lips touch the tip of his muzzle. Her kiss felt wonderful, but he had to concentrate to make sure his tongue didn't dart out.

She caressed his face then climbed out of bed. She quickly got dressed.

"I wish I could spend all day lying with you, but I have to go see my queen."

"I understand. I am sure my father could use some help. I will go see him."

He watched her leave the room then he got dressed. He quickly went to the door when someone knocked loudly on it.

"I saw your female walking by so I knew it was safe to come to your chamber," Zenith said.

"I am heading to the healing quarter. You are welcome to join me."

"Alright. So, have you been challenged yet?"

"No." Ramiro started walking down the corridor. "I heard you have been challenged a lot."

"Yeah, the older warriors think they can easily defeat me. So far, none has and none will."

"I am sure with your skill they won't."

"Ramiro!"

Ramiro turned around and saw a large male coming toward him. "What is it?"

"You are lucky you are the son of Tomar or I would take your female from you."

"If you wish to challenge me then do so."

"You are Tomar's son. I have too much respect for him to injure his offspring. There are more than enough Rundal females why didn't you choose one of them?"

Ramiro drew his sword. "Either challenge me for my female or keep moving. I won't be badgered by you."

Mara hurried back to Ramiro. She heard the commotion and even though she should hurry to her queen she couldn't leave Ramiro alone with an anger barbarian male.

"Those Loma females are strange. First they want those weaker pathetic males, now this one…" he motioned his head to Mara, "…wants to bed a lizard. What's wrong is a barbarian male's cock too big for you?"

Ramiro shoved the large warrior away from Mara. "Draw your sword," Ramiro growled.

"It's okay Ramiro, this ox's words mean nothing to me."

"Draw your sword!"

"Come here," Zenith said as he gently grabbed Mara's hand and pulled her over to the side.

"No, stop this please," Mara said, pleading with Zenith to help Ramiro.

"I can't interfere. That barbarian male wanted to anger Ramiro. Have faith that your male can protect you."

Mara watched Ramiro fight with the barbarian. Their fighting styles were so different. Ramiro was more agile while the barbarian was stronger.

"I have trained with Ramiro. He will defeat this hot tempered barbarian," Zenith said. "His speed is his greatest asset and he uses it well. Plus, see how he uses his tail. It is almost like a third arm. The Rundal could be magnificent fighters if they weren't so peaceful at heart."

Ramiro easily defeated his opponent. It took all of his restraint not to kill the male for talking to Mara like that.

"Wow," Mara said. She had never actually seen a Rundal male fight before. It was almost like watching music coming to life. Sure she has seen the Rundal males train, but never has seen them fight.

"See, if the Rundal had the barbarian's battle lust they would make very formidable opponents," Zenith said.

"I am sorry you had to endure that," Ramiro said to Mara.

"Words don't wound me, Ramiro. My spirit is stronger than that. You fought well, very well." She smiled at him. "Thank you my male for defending my honor."

Ramiro didn't know what to say. He grabbed her hand and brought it up to his muzzle where he nuzzled her hand.

"I knew you had it in you. Now if you could use those sharp teeth of yours, damn you would be so fierce," Zenith said.

"That is what I told him. He should use everything the Goddess has given him," Mara added.

Ramiro grabbed her hand and started to walk. "Come on let's get going. Zenith where is your female?"

"She is with her queen. There are several Rundal males there so I don't fear for my female's safety."

"You trust a Rundal warrior that much, huh?" Ramiro asked.

"Of course."

"I must go to my queen too. I will be okay."

"Hurry there alright?"

"I will, my male."

Zenith waited for her to leave. "You do love her don't you? I can see it in your eyes. Tell me, do you see my love for Petra in my eyes."

"Yes."

"We will be going through the joining ceremony together if we manage to hold on to our females. I like that. Then our offspring can play together…oh, I'm sorry I…forgot that…"

"Don't worry about it. Besides, Mara has come up with a plan for us to still raise offspring. So see our offspring can play together."

"Niro wants me to move to Dascon so I can train Zenos full time. Do you think you will be able to be stationed here as well?"

"I am sure that won't be a problem. Alamaxa will probably throw me out of the Rundal village when he becomes ruler, which is what I want to talk with father about. I heard that he wants to step down as ruler."

"That is his decision."

"I know, but he has proven to be a grand ruler for our people. Will Alamaxa be a good ruler? I don't know. I guess we will see. I like it here in Dascon anyways. I am sure Mara probably would want to stay with Petra and Fenalla. So it all works out for the best anyways."

"But you are the Grand General of your warriors."

"Alamaxa would probably want to take over that role too. Niro has wanted a Rundal general stationed here for some time. Maybe I can see if I am worthy enough to become what he wants."

"You are the Grand General of your people. I think you are worthy enough."

"I will discuss this with father. One more week and Mara will be my mate and Petra will be yours."

"I know I can't wait. Let's get this talking done with your father then you can spar with me on the training grounds."

"Alright."

Chapter Nineteen

It had been a long hard week, but Zenith managed to fight off all challengers for Petra. This impressed Niro a great deal and strengthened his belief in the young warrior. He was certain now that Zenith was the warrior he wanted to train his son.

Ramiro wasn't challenged but that once. Out of respect for Tomar no barbarian wanted to chance hurting Ramiro.

"Who is this Alistair?" Petra said as she watched Zenith getting dressed.

"He is the ruler of the Larmat clan. Remember I told you about him."

"He is coming here just for the joining ceremony?"

"Yep, he is bringing the Larmat warriors who successfully protected their mates so they can join in the ceremony as well."

"All of the Loma warriors have mates?"

"Yes. It's been crazy around here with so many protectors. It's such a glorious day for my people and yours as well. With so many couples the number of offspring should be many next year."

"Tomar is going to do the ceremony I heard."

"The joining ceremony is a bit different this year. With so many couples being joined from all three races I guess it makes sense."

"My queen has told me that Alamaxa is coming to the joining ceremony too."

"Really…poor Ramiro."

"It may not be so bad for Ramiro. You know seeing how much he makes Mara happy I feel awful for wanting them not to be together."

Zenith walked over to her and pulled the sheet off of her. He let his eyes linger over her beautiful body.

"We just made love several times already aren't you going to be late for your training session with Zenos."

Her body heated up seeing that look of lust on his face.

Zenith jumped on the bed and pinned her under him. He untied his loincloth and pulled it from his body.

"Fight me," he growled. "Try to dominate me, my warrior female."

Her body ignited with a burning passion, the thought of dominating such a strong male made her body quiver. She wrapped her legs around him and flipped him over so now she was on top.

"It won't be that easy."

His cock rubbed against her clit distracting her briefly. He flipped her over again and used his body weight to pin her to the bed.

"You are too distracting, my beautiful male."

"If you don't defeat me then I won't give you my cock." He rubbed his cock against her. He knew damn well he was going to fuck her whether she won or not, but he wanted to tease, and tempt her. He talked with Mara about the customs of the Loma warriors. They truly enjoyed dominating their males. Problem was a barbarian male loved to dominate his female. The more he thought about them erotic wrestling for dominance the harder his cock became.

She surprised him when she broke free and knocked him off the bed.

"You are not denying me that glorious cock of yours. I will take what I want."

"We'll see about that."

He sprung back up to his feet as she charged at him. She swept her leg knocking him to the ground again. Before he could jump back up she climbed on top of him. She held him with all her strength.

It took him a moment but he managed to push her off. He grabbed her legs and pulled her to him. Using his legs he held her tightly by the upper waist. Her face was buried in his stomach as he pinned her arms behind her.

"Give up," he cooed.

"Not yet." She licked at his stomach.

"That won't work. Now do you give up?" He squeezed his legs tighter.

She rubbed her breasts against his hard cock.

He loosened his hold on her arms. She managed to free her arms. She pushed her body down just enough so she could take the head of his cock into her mouth. He used his legs to roll her onto her back. He felt her arms go around his waist as she pulled him closer so she could take more of his cock into her mouth. He reached under him and grabbed her hair. He pulled hard as he began thrusting his cock into her mouth. After a few moments he grabbed her arms and pinned them above her head as he continued to thrust.

"Is this what you wanted, female," he growled as he thrust harder into her mouth. "Is it?!"

She responded by sucking harder.

He rolled off of her then grabbed a hold of her, flipping her over. She started to struggle. He wasn't going to take her that easy.

Zenith felt a frenzy building inside of him. Something he had never felt before. He wanted to take her so badly he couldn't contain himself. He was going to have her no matter how hard she fought.

"Petra...I can't stop this," he growled.

He wrestled her back to the floor grabbing her hair pushing her head to the ground. She tried to fight but he had her in such an awkward position.

"I will take you now, female. Submit to me. I don't want to hurt you."

"No, you want me then fight for it."

The frenzy exploded inside Zenith and he couldn't stop himself. He used all his strength to pin her under him. He lifted her hips and drove his cock into her. He thrust hard and urgent. He pulled her hair and bent over biting her shoulder hard. He growled and grunted as he drove himself into her harder and harder. He arched back and howled as his orgasm exploded. As soon as he came down from the heights of pleasure his cock grew hard again with the same urgent need. This frenzy wouldn't ebb. He took her over and over, more and more animalistic each time he took her. Finally, the frenzy stopped. He lay on the floor exhausted.

"What was that?!" Petra said winded.

"I don't know. I couldn't stop fucking you. It was an all consuming need."

"Is this normal for your people?"

"I don't know. My father never told me anything about mating." Zenith quickly sat up and looked at her. "I didn't hurt you did I?"

"No, but you sure wore me out. You better get ready. You are going to be late for your training session."

"Are you sure I didn't hurt you?"

"I'm sure, in fact I wonder if I can make that happen again. That was wonderful. Mmm, my male you were so strong, so…I better stop now I don't think my pussy can take anymore right now."

Zenith quickly got dressed then left the chamber. Before he left he checked over her body to make sure he didn't hurt her. He hoped Zenos would understand if he was a little late. He had to talk to Tomar to see what that frenzy was and more importantly was it going to get worse. He couldn't risk hurting Petra.

Zenith stood awkwardly in the healing ward as he waited for Tomar.

"What is troubling you, Zenith?" Tomar said as he walked into the room.

"May I speak with you alone?" He looked at the other Rundal males.

"Of course." Tomar signaled for the other males to leave.

"This is going to sound strange."

Tomar could see that Zenith was embarrassed by whatever he wanted to tell him. "Just come out and say it. It will be easier on you."

"When I was mating with my female...this strange, urgent need overcame me. I...ended up taking her over and over...I...umm..."

"Oh...the frenzy."

Zenith quickly looked into Tomar's face. "You know what this is?"

"I am surprised that your father or at least your mother didn't speak to you about this. You have nothing to worry about. It seems that when you barbarian males get teased or overly excited a frenzy may be sparked. This is normal."

"But what if I hurt Petra?"

"It is rare that a male does any lasting damage to his mate during his frenzy. The female usually submits to him and gives him what he needs to calm his frenzy. You may want to speak with your female and tell her this. The less she fights the less chance she will be hurt."

"I feel better now. I didn't understand what was happening."

"I keep forgetting just how young you are. If you have anymore questions I am always happy to help."

"Thank you, Tomar. I'm sorry but I must hurry to the training grounds. I don't want to keep Zenos waiting too long."

"I understand." Tomar watched Zenith hurry from the room. He smiled and started to chuckle, poor Zenith that had to be awkward for him. Tomar headed out of the chamber toward the ship dock. Alistair and Alamaxa were arriving today.

ഇഇഇ

"Oh my goodness," Robin exclaimed as she saw Alamaxa coming down the boarding ramp.

"What's wrong, my female?" Niro said.

"Is that Alamaxa? He is so large and he sure doesn't have that peaceful look Tomar has about him."

"I am assuming that's him. See the Rundal guards flanking him. That Rundal female with him must be his mate."

"Where?"

"The small Rundal female behind him. She is really adorned with many jewels."

"She is beautiful for a Rundal. Sasha never wore such elaborate coverings."

"I suspect Alamaxa requested his female to dress like that."

"I don't know, Niro. He kind of scares me."

"Don't worry I will protect you."

"I know you will." Robin wrapped her arms around one of his arms.

"Whoa, Daddy is that the new Rundal leader?" Zenos asked as Laigne brought him and Rose over to Robin.

"I think so, son. Show him respect."

"I will Daddy."

"How did your training go this afternoon?"

"Zenith was late, but he stayed longer. I learned to double slash and block series of slash attacks."

"Very good."

"Did you get hurt?" Robin asked.

"Of course not Mommy, Zenith is very careful."

"Ah, I see my son has arrived. Come let me introduce you," Tomar said as he approached Niro.

"Niro…that is Alamaxa," Robin said holding his arm tighter.

"It is okay, little one." Niro patted her hand then led her to Alamaxa.

"Father." Alamaxa bowed his head to Tomar.

"Alamaxa let me introduce you to Niro, his mate Robin, and their offspring Zenos and Rose."

"It is a great honor to finally meet you, Niro."

"Like wise," Niro responded.

"This is my mate Lei and this is my son Taran."

Niro nodded his head toward them. "Robin, please escort Alamaxa's family to their chamber. I would like to show him around."

"Alright." Robin walked over to Lei. "Please follow me."

Taran looked to be the same age as Rose. It was a bit harder to tell with Rundal offspring.

"Zenos, you help protect them," Niro said.

"I will, Sir."

"I see your son has already started his training. Mine is still a bit too young."

"Zenith started training him when Zenos was four summers old."

"This is good to see. Zenos will be your next ruler." Alamaxa liked Niro instantly. It was good to see a ruler who looked and acted strong. "I wish to show my respects to your mother, Niro. Is she still among the living?"

"Yes, I would be happy to introduce you. She has been busy making Queen Rhaya feel at home."

"Your father Hakan was a great leader. It is a shame I didn't get to meet him before he took the great journey."

"Tomar please join us."

"Certainly."

ഇയഇയഇയ

"Tell me when Alistair is going to arrive," Lei said as they entered the guest chamber of the leader hut.

"He should be here later on today."

"I am most curious to see the offspring of a Larmat male and Dascon female."

"I will be certain to introduce you."

Robin didn't feel as comfortable around Lei as she did around Sasha. Lei was royalty and she knew it. Sasha was warm and friendly to everyone.

"Taran come here. You know your father doesn't want you wandering off."

"Is Taran your only offspring?"

"So far, but I will be giving my male many more offspring. I am tired from the journey I would like to rest now."

"Come on Zenos and Rose let's leave them to get settle in." Robin lifted Rose up into her arms and they left the chamber and headed to theirs.

"Mom, that Rundal female isn't very friendly. I like Sasha better."

"So do I, Zenos. However, we still have to be nice to her. Her male is going to be the next ruler of the Rundal people."

"He is scary. I have never seen a Rundal male so large before. Tomar is very nice I wish he would stay the ruler. Do you think daddy will like Alamaxa?"

"I don't know. It doesn't matter whether Niro likes him or not. He will have to still get along with him."

"Why isn't Ramiro going to be the new leader? He is just as smart and nice as Tomar."

"Alamaxa is older."

"Still, I wish Ramiro was going to be the new leader." Zenos stopped and placed himself in front of Robin. Two large Dascon warriors quickly ran up and drew their swords. The larger one gently pushed Zenos back.

"Niro's mate stay there," one said.

"What's going on?"

"Larmat warriors," one growled.

"Put those swords away. What's the matter with you. Zenos, I told you that the Larmat warriors are our friends now."

"Robin!" Anne rushed over.

Robin's guards parted allowing her to pass.

"Anne, it's good to see you again. Where's Alistair?"

"He is down by the conja stables, he should be with Niro and some really big Rundal male."

"The Rundal male is Alamaxa."

"Damn…he is a big one."

"Come on let's go back to my chamber. You can tell me what you have been up to. Oh…" Robin set Rose down then placed her hand on Anne's rounded belly. "When are you due?"

"Not for awhile. Can you believe I am only four months pregnant. Alistair was so worried about me flying on the conja all the way up here, but there is no way I was going to miss my chance to see everyone."

"Petra come here." Robin motioned to her.

"What is it Niro's mate."

"Please call me Robin."

Petra looked at the woman with ebony skin who was standing next to Robin. She never saw that shade of skin before on a human female.

"This is Alistair's mate Anne. She is from Earth."

"How many shades of skin are there on Earth females?"

"There is quite a range of shades."

"Interesting."

"Anne, this is Petra, she is going to be Zenith's mate. She is a warrior from the planet Loma."

"It is so nice to meet you. To be honest I was quite eager to meet you warrior women. Wow, you are big girls aren't you. Remind me to never make you angry."

Petra just looked at her with a puzzled look.

"Remember they are like the people of Malka," Robin said to Anne.

"I am most eager to meet your mate Alistair." Petra looked at the two large blond males who were standing behind Anne. "They don't look like Zenith."

"Oh, these are Larmat warriors."

Petra walked over to one and grabbed a strand of his golden hair. "The color of the noon sun."

"Petra!" Zenith growled as he drew his sword. "Get away from that male."

"Calm yourself young warrior," the Larmat male said.

"Hey, there is no need for drama. These two Larmat warriors have mates already. Your female was just curious," Anne said.

"Zenith put your sword away."

"Do not draw your sword in front of my mate again."

Zenith quickly turned around and saw Alistair standing right behind him. "Forgive me, Alistair." Zenith sheathed his sword and backed away.

Petra hurried to Zenith. Her eyes were glued on Alistair. He did look like a mix of the two different clans. His light brown hair and pale blue eyes were testament to that. He carried himself like Niro did which was most impressive.

"Alistair, it is so good to see you." Robin went over to him and shook his hand. She wanted to give him a hug but Niro would not stand for her touching another male like that.

"You look happy." He smiled at her. "Where is Niro?"

"He will be here soon. He is showing Alamaxa around. Anne, didn't you say Alistair was with Niro already."

"I assumed he was. I saw Niro and that Rundal male heading toward the conja stables."

"Really, I am most eager to meet this Alamaxa."

"Oh baby, he is one big Rundal male. I saw him. He looks like he would bite your head off without even thinking about it."

"Now I am even more eager to meet him. Tomar is here as well?"

"Yes."

"Good, I would like him to check Anne and make sure she is alright."

"I am fine. How many times do I need to say this. The Rundal healer in Larmat told you this too. Robin, Alistair is driving me nuts being so overprotective of me."

"I hear you. Niro about drove me crazy when I was pregnant."

"Alistair, please follow me," a Dascon male said as he approached. "Niro wishes for you to join him and the others."

"Anne, stay with Robin."

"Don't worry about me."

Alistair walked over and pulled Anne into his arms. He kissed her softly then caressed her hair. "Guards, don't let her out of your sight."

"Yes, Alistair."

"I will be back soon."

"Take your time. You have to get to know Alamaxa. I will stay with Robin. I won't go anywhere without my guards. I promise."

Alistair smiled at her then walked away.

"He is like Niro," Petra said.

"Petra, we have to guard our queen. Niro has summoned her to join him and the other two leaders," Mara said as she hurried over. Ramiro was right behind her.

"Zenith…"

"Go, my warrior female." He wanted to tell her that he was coming to protect her. But he couldn't. Her queen summoned her. She is a warrior after all. He held his worry inside. He could see her face light up with a warrior's pride. He can't take that away from her.

"I will be back soon. Where will you be?"

"I will be with Zenos."

Ramiro walked over to Zenith as the women hurried off. "That must have been hard for you."

"Yeah it was."

Chapter Twenty

Rhaya sat at the large table with Niro, Alamaxa, Tomar and Alistair. They had been talking about the joining ceremony. Niro had made it a point to include her with the decision-making. Her greatest fear was that Niro would take away her rule of her own people once they got here. But to her surprise he didn't. He even made it a point to ask her about their customs. And this morning he showed her the plans for the temple to the Loma Goddess that he planned to build just outside the village. She hadn't asked for any of this. He just did it all on his own. Now, he was treating her like the ruler she was in front of these other three males. The empress feared Niro. So much so she called a council of all the rulers of every village. Rhaya was sure now that the empress planned to have Tomar recreate the disease so she could use it as a weapon against Niro's warriors.

"Rhaya, what is the Loma custom of joining?" Niro asked, drawing her attention back to the meeting.

"Our custom is very simple. A priestess announces to the Goddess the joining of the female and male. That's it."

"You said you brought two of your priestesses right. I remembered that because you said these priestesses couldn't have male mates."

"That's correct."

"Tomar, please make certain that at least one of these priestesses is at the joining ceremony."

"Thank you, Niro."

"It is only fair that your people be joined in your custom as well. As far as Ramiro is concern…"

"Ramiro will be joined in the barbarian custom," Alamaxa said.

"Alamaxa, this has not been decided," Tomar said.

"If he wants a human female then he should be joined as one. I can't believe that you are allowing him to do this in the first place."

"It will be up to Ramiro to decide. This is my decision," Tomar firmly said.

"What is the Rundal custom of joining?" Rhaya asked.

"The female accepts the male publicly. This is done by standing by each one saying I take you as my mate. Then they intertwine tails. Tell me Father how is Mara going to do this with Ramiro. This whole thing is a folly. Ramiro should take a Rundal mate. He is one of the perfect specimens of a Rundal male, hell he is second only to me."

"His choice has been made. He has gone through the barbarian trial of protection. He has proven himself worthy of his female."

"I heard none of Niro's warriors but one challenged him out of their respect for you. How is this proving himself worthy?"

"In the eyes of my people if he has protected his mate from the other warriors he is worthy. Since no warrior has challenged him, but the one, he had it easy, but still he proved himself," Niro added. He could see Alamaxa's strength, but he lacked the compassion Tomar had. In time, perhaps, Alamaxa could learn compassion.

"When is the joining ceremony?" Rhaya asked.

"Tomorrow. We are eliminating the joining feast because your warriors won't understand the meaning. This is where the male and female perform the dance of seduction. There is no need to get into it since it won't happen this time."

"This is a joyous time for all of Malka. A new hope for the barbarians as well as the Loma warriors." Tomar lifted his glass in a toast.

"What about our people?" Alamaxa asked.

"It's a new beginning for all."

ഇ൝ഇ൝

Alistair watched Mara and Ramiro walking together out onto the training grounds. "That is a strange sight," he said to Demos.

"Yes, it is."

"They will have a tough time. The prejudice they will endure will be plentiful I am sure."

"That Loma warrior is strong and Ramiro has walked with our people for so long he will bend the people's will to his way of thinking. In my opinion he should have succeeded Tomar. He understands both the barbarian and Rundal ways. Now that his mate will be a Loma warrior he will soon know their ways as well."

"I agree with you. I am having trouble understanding Alamaxa. There is so much anger in his heart. I don't understand where it is coming from."

"He probably believes his father has given in too much to our people. After all he was locked up in the Rundal village all his life. The training to be a Rundal leader is very intense. Maybe when he sees how much our people benefit each other his anger will cool."

"What if it don't? I have no wish to war with the Rundal."

"I have faith that Tomar will know when to give control over to his son. I doubt he would while Alamaxa has so much anger seething inside."

"You're right. Niro is with Tomar and Alamaxa now. They are explaining everything to Alamaxa."

"This is a good thing. Niro will show Alamaxa what our people mean to each other."

"I heard Nina is having two babies."

"Yes, she is," Demos said with pride in his voice. "And I see Anne is carrying your baby."

"Our offspring will have to play with each other. Tomar has told me that Anne is giving me a son."

"Nina is giving me a son and a daughter."

"There is much to celebrate tomorrow."

"Yes there is. Now draw your sword. I haven't had the pleasure of beating you at a sparring match in awhile."

"And you won't have that pleasure today." Alistair drew his sword and rushed at Demos.

Chapter Twenty-One

Petra fussed with the long white covering she wore. "Why can't we wear our battle outfits?"

"This is the barbarian custom. We must try to be as beautiful as we can for our males," Mara added.

"I like the way the silky fabric feels against my skin," Fenalla said.

The barbarian females finished putting the jewels in the Loma warriors' hair.

"It feels strange having so much adornment on," Petra said as she looked in the mirror.

"You look beautiful. Zenith will love it."

"I'm sure he will. He gets to wear his full battle covering."

"And won't he look fierce," Mara said.

"Is Ramiro dressing like the barbarians?"

"I think he is wearing the priestly robes of his father."

"Really?" Fenalla said.

"He was deciding when I last seen him."

"I have seen a Rundal male wearing the white and gold robes of the priest. It was more fitting than the barbarian coverings they usually wear," Fenalla said.

"What about Laigne? What is he wearing?"

"He said he is coming as himself. It would look silly for him to wear full battle armor since he is not a warrior. I imagine he will wear the plain coverings of a weaker male. It doesn't matter to me, just as long as he becomes my mate."

"It looks like a sea of white and gold," Petra said as they stepped out onto the training grounds."

"Well there are at least one hundred and forty Loma warriors getting mates today. There are also Rundal females getting joined with their Rundal males today as well."

"You look beautiful, my female."

Petra quickly turned to the sound of Zenith's voice. Her breath caught seeing him standing there in his full battle dress. He wore a black leather loincloth with strips of brown leather criss-crossing his chest. He had two golden bracelets on and a golden headband. His sword was strapped to his back and he had a dagger in its sheath strapped to his right thigh.

"My male." She smiled.

"You look fierce," Ramiro said to Zenith. "And your female is most beautiful."

"You look like a Rundal priest." Zenith looked at the long white and gold robe Ramiro wore.

"This is how a Rundal male dresses when declaring a female his mate."

"Oh. It suits you."

"Mara…" Ramiro just stared at her. Her beauty robbed him of any rational thought.

"Ramiro." She walked over to him and gently took his claw.

"Are you sure you want me as a mate?"

"More than anything."

"Then come. Zenith, Niro wishes us to be on the stage. You as well Fenalla, Laigne is with Robin he will be here shortly."

They all walked to the stage. The air was filled with so much happiness and hope that it made a peace fill everyone.

"Tomar, look at our son," Sasha said as she watched Ramiro walk up onto the stage.

"He is so happy. Did he tell you what his female wants to do?"

"No."

"She wants to adopt the abandon weaker male children from the Larmat villages. And she wants to take in the orphan Rundal hatchlings."

"She does? I didn't know that."

"We must ready the sacred juice for the barbarian males to drink."

"I have taken care of that. Once the ceremony is over the males will line up and be given the juice to drink."

"Alamaxa is only here out of duty." Tomar looked over at Alamaxa sitting on the special chairs Niro had set up for the leaders.

"He will learn all that is involved in ruling our people."

"Until he does I can't step down."

"I have faith that you will know when the time is right."

"There are so many," Robin said as she and Niro approach Tomar.

"Isn't this a joyous time," Sasha said.

"Oh yes," Niro added.

"Laigne, I wish you all the happiness in the world," Robin said as she hugged him tightly. "You are always welcome to visit me and the children." She placed a golden headband on him.

"No, only a warrior wears this."

"Please, I wish for you to have something special on your joining day. Here comes your female. Fenalla you look beautiful."

"Thank you." Fenalla couldn't take her eyes off of Laigne. He was dressed in his simple weaker male covering, but the golden headband illuminated his dark eyes.

Laigne grabbed her hand and walked over to where Zenith and the others were standing.

Tomar started the ceremony. "We have three different cultures represented here at this wondrous occasion. In the words of the Loma warriors…"

A chorus of female voices declaring their devotion to the males rang out.

"In the words of the barbarian warriors."

Zenith gently took Petra's hand and placed one of his bracelets on her arm. He squeezed it gently to secure it. "I take you as my mate. I swear my love, life and protection to you and all our future offspring."

Tomar had shortened the traditional barbarian ceremony, but the meaning was still there.

"In the words of the Rundal."

"I take you as my male. I say for all those who can hear," Mara said.

"I take you as my female. I say for all those who can hear," Ramiro said.

Ramiro lifted his tail intertwining with her arm. "A symbol of our unity, we are now one soul."

"To the Goddess of the barbarian, to the Goddess of the Loma, and to the Goddess of the Rundal I declare all who have spoken the sacred joining words are now and will be forever joined as one soul to their mate," Tomar said.

Zenith kissed Petra then took the cup of sacred juice offered by the Rundal priest. He drank it down.

The Loma priestesses and the Rundal priest passed out the sacred juice to all the barbarian males.

"Now let the feast of celebration begin!" Niro cried out.

After the feast and all of the couples went off with each other Robin walked back to the leader hut with Niro. He held her hand in his as they leisurely strolled.

"So many new couples," Robin said.

"Next year there will be a lot of offspring born."

"You look so happy."

"How could I not be. There is hope for my people and I am here with you, my female."

"I love you, Niro."

"You warm my heart, little one."

Robin squeezed his hand harder.

"Is Zenith going to move here to train Zenos full time?"

"Yes and Ramiro will be the first Rundal general stationed at Dascon."

"I see that Alamaxa has already left."

"He left quite a while ago. Tomar has much to teach him before he can rule the Rundal effectively. I trust Tomar without question. He will know when his son is ready to lead."

"You know I feel sorry for Nina."

"Why?"

"She is having two babies at one time. That poor thing, I hope she will be able to carry them to term."

"Tomar said she was strong. The only real problem is getting her to stop training for awhile."

"I am sure Demos will convince her."

"I will probably be sparring with him a lot in these coming months."

"Why?"

"Tomar told him that he had to take it easy on Nina. They can't mate as much."

"Oh boy, you will be sparring with him a lot." Robin chuckled. "I am happy for Laigne. I hope he and Fenalla have a happy life together. Thank you for allowing them to be joined."

"He fought for her. He had no chance against the warrior, yet he kept getting up and fighting. He earned the right to have that female. But it warms my heart to see you so happy about it."

"You are a good ruler, Niro. I have seen what you have done for the Loma people. You allowed them to keep their traditions."

"It would be unjust not to. It is the same with the Larmat clan. I can't force the Dascon way on these people."

"Hakan would be so proud of you. I am proud to be your mate."

"As I am proud to be yours, little one."

"Your mother seems to really like Queen Rhaya."

"I am glad for that."

"Now what will you do for females?"

"For now I will have Tomar gather some more Earth women. And he is already searching for another compatible planet to seek out females. I feel there will be more female offspring born now that the Loma genes will mingle with the Malka."

Niro scooped up Robin into his arms. "My mother is watching Zenos and Rose. We have all night. Mmm, all the wicked thoughts that are flooding my mind is making my cock ache."

"Then hurry up and take me to our chamber. I got a few wicked thoughts of my own." Robin squealed and held on for dear life when Niro started to run still holding her in his arms.

The End

Justus Roux's website has excerpts of all her novels, short stories written by Justus and several talented guest writers and poets. There is a monthly contest for a chance to win one of Justus Roux's novels. Plus much more

Come visit Justus at www.justusroux.com

Printed in the United States
90501LV00001B/19/A

9 780979 744402